"**Let go of me,**" she
raged. "**Are you mad?**"

Helen struck at Damon's hand on her
knee as his other arm pulled her
against him.

"No, I'm not mad," he said. "Just
curious about this much-vaunted
permissive society of yours, Eleni.
Stop fluttering, little bird, and show
me how a liberated woman behaves
with her man."

Lean fingers encircled her slender
wrists, pinioning them securely, and
his dark head bent until his mouth
touched the hollow of her throat. She
gasped with helplessness and fright,
and another subtler emotion that
she could not understand.

"No—Damon—please," she said
imploringly as his thumb stroked the
soft nape of her neck, sending
strange tremors through her body.

"I want to see more, *kóugla mou*."
His voice roughened. "I want to see all
of you."

SARA CRAVEN
is also the author of these

Harlequin Presents

and this

Harlequin Romance

Many of these titles are available at your local bookseller.

For a free catalogue listing all available Harlequin Romances and Harlequin Presents, send your name and address to:

HARLEQUIN READER SERVICE,
M.P.O. Box 707, Niagara Falls, NY 14302
Canadian address: Stratford, Ontario N5A 6W2

SARA CRAVEN

moon of aphrodite

Harlequin Books

TORONTO • LONDON • LOS ANGELES • AMSTERDAM
SYDNEY • HAMBURG • PARIS • STOCKHOLM • ATHENS • TOKYO

Harlequin Presents edition published February 1981
ISBN 0-373-10411-1

Original hardcover edition published in 1980
by Mills & Boon Limited

CHAPTER ONE

"I'M NOT GOING and that's final," Helen said.

Hugo Brandon gave a worried sigh and pushed a hand through his thick thatch of graying hair. The letter lay between them on the breakfast table, flimsy, foreign looking, the handwriting spiky and black, managing to convey an impression of autocracy.

He said, "Don't be too hasty, darling."

"Too hasty?" Helen's eyes flashed fire. "Dad—you can't be serious. After the way he treated you and mother—cutting her off completely like that. Refusing all communication, even when she was so ill and begged him to write and say she was forgiven?"

Her father was silent, staring down at the tablecloth, his fingers drawing a restless pattern on it.

She said, "Or that's what you've always told me, dad, dozens of times. Are you going to say now that it wasn't true?"

"Oh, it was true. And more." Hugo's voice was heavy. "But he's an old man, Helen. A sick old man. You're his only grandchild. And he wants to see you. It isn't that extraordinary."

"My God," Helen said explosively, and there was a tense silence.

The letter from Grandfather Korialis had come like a bolt from the blue. Helen had read it twice and she still could hardly believe the contents. For nearly nineteen years, her Greek grandfather had chosen to forget her existence. He had not even acknowledged the news of her birth. And now this demand for her presence at his villa on the island of Phoros just off the Greek mainland. Surely he couldn't really believe that after all this time, all this bitterness, she would simply present herself to order.

But perhaps he did. Perhaps when you owned a chain of hotels like Michael Korialis, when you said "Jump," everyone jumped.

Well, she, Helen, was neither his employee nor beholden to him in any way. On the contrary, she thought broodingly. She would be the exception to the Korialis rule. She would not jump.

Hugo said gently, "Has it occurred to you to think what your mother would have wanted you to do?"

Helen had a brief unhappy image of her mother not long before her death six years previously, the sweet high cheekbones, which Helen had inherited, thrown into prominence by the haggard thinness of her face.

She knew what Maria Brandon would have wanted— *had* wanted all her married life, happy though it had been. She had wanted to be reconciled with the stern man in Greece who had cast her off from him completely when she had defied him and the marriage he had arranged for her and eloped with the tall English artist who had been staying in a nearby village.

She knew that if it had been to her mother that this unexpected olive branch had been extended, then she would have accepted it without a second thought, and joyfully, too.

But I'm not capable of that kind of generosity, Helen told herself flatly. *After years of slights and neglect, I can't just perform an about-face and pretend that it all never happened. All this time he's ignored the fact that I'm alive. Now he wants to see me. It makes no sense.*

But at the same time, having read her grandfather's letter, she was uneasily aware that it made all the sense in the world. The letter had not been long, but it had been very much to the point.

He had suffered a severe heart attack, he wrote, and wished before he died to see his only grandchild. An airplane ticket to Athens would be provided, transport to the island arranged, and all expenses met. He would expect her to stay at his villa for a minimum of one month.

The tone of the letter had been so much like a business contract that she had almost looked for the inevitable dotted line on which to sign.

She glanced up and saw her father watching her, his face grave and a little compassionate, as if he sensed her inner struggle.

She said reproachfully, "You're not being fair. But it makes no difference. Even if I wanted to go—and I don't—it wouldn't be possible. We're coming up to the height of the tourist season, and you know how busy the gallery becomes."

Hugo nodded. "I know, but I'd be prepared to release you, and find another assistant, if you were willing to go to Phoros."

"I don't understand you." She spread her hands helplessly.

"I'm not sure I understand myself," he admitted. "I only know that I'm tired of the bitterness and enmity, and that this seems a good way to end them once and for all. But if you really feel that you can't do it, then I won't press you. The ultimate decision must be yours."

"If he'd only invited you as well. . . ." she began, but he cut across her with a wry smile.

"Now that really would be impossible for all sorts of reasons. It's you he wants to see. Maria's daughter."

"I feel I'm being blackmailed," she said in a low voice. "Not very subtle pressure is being applied and I don't like it." Her voice deepened passionately. "After all, he didn't respond when mother was so ill."

"Your mother underplayed the seriousness of the situation, perhaps deliberately, I don't know. She always made excuses for him and his actions all her life. Perhaps she was letting him down lightly for the last time."

Helen said yes almost absently. Her hand reached for the letter, screwing it into a ball. Her eyes met her father's in defiance and appeal. "I may look like her, dad, but I haven't her forgiving nature. He may be a wealthy and a powerful man, but he can't come and go in our lives just as he pleases."

"Are you prepared to tell him so?" Hugo's voice was gentle and without censure.

"I don't intend to reply at all." She tossed the ball of paper into the waste bin. "Problem disposed of. Now let's change to a happier topic. Did you get the message from Paul that I left for you last night?"

"Yes." Her father smiled. "And I've telephoned him. He's been working really hard, and the exhibition won't have to be postponed after all."

"It never does have to be postponed," Helen smiled in response. "It's just eleventh-hour panic on his part. God knows why. Or you do, perhaps?"

"I have an idea," Hugo said. "Though I must admit no one ever clamored to put on an exhibition of my work."

Helen gave him an affectionate smile before rising to busy herself clearing the breakfast things from the table. Her father's work, as far as she could judge, had been competent but not outstanding, but he possessed the eye of a judge, a connoisseur where other people's painting was concerned. He was also a realistic man, and had recognized quite early in his career that he would probably never earn enough from painting alone to support himself, plus a wife and child. A legacy from an uncle had enabled him to buy a share in a gallery near the

West End. The Gallery wasn't doing too well, but Hugo Brandon had changed all that, and within five years he had been able to buy his partner out and replace the gallery's rather pretentious name with the single word Brandon. He made a name for himself on both sides of the Atlantic, Europe included, as a man who could spot a real talent in the making. And Helen had never asked anything better than to join him in his work.

But sometimes she wondered if he ever regretted that it was not his own signature that his customers sought on their canvases. Was he happy, she thought. Was he fulfilled, or had he settled for second best? She hoped not, but doubted whether she would ever know the truth.

One thing she had never doubted was his love for her, and for his late wife. But again she wondered if he would have worked quite so hard to make the gallery a success financially as well as artistically if he had not married a rich man's daughter. Perhaps he had been determined that Maria would never count the cost of all she had given up in order to become his wife.

God, she thought ruefully as she stacked dishes in the drying rack, *everything's so complicated. Except for my life,* she amended hastily.

Helen had enjoyed the years since she had left school. She liked the fact that their apartment was sited immediately over the gallery, as well as the work she did there. She was beginning to be a good saleswoman, and learning about art, as well, which pleased her. And without being conceited, she was aware that her own attractions—a slim body with rounded breasts and hips, an oval face with high cheekbones, and clear hazel eyes fringed by lashes shades darker than her honey-blond hair—contributed to success.

Her mother had been blond, too, but her eyes had been brown like pansies, and full of laughter.

Helen's eyes darkened, too, when she was angry, which was really the only form of passion she had ever encountered. She had never lacked for men to take her out, but her romances so far had been very tentative affairs with little commitment on either side.

Her thoughts for a moment went to Christopher who was taking her out that very evening. She liked him, she enjoyed his kisses even, but something warned her that was all the involvement she wanted, although she was aware his own desire was for a much closer relationship.

Perhaps in time, she thought almost absently, then caught herself. What was she thinking of? Her mother had preached few moral lessons at her, perhaps because she guessed the morality her daughter would be subjected to would be a very different thing from her own sheltered girlhood in Greece. Yet one thing she had stressed—without love, there could not, should not be any giving. And Helen had to admit she could not imagine love blossoming from anything as lukewarm as her present feelings for Christopher. Like most of the other young men who had passed briefly through her life he was a pleasant companion, but little more.

She sighed faintly. Perhaps this was why their passage was so fleeting. Maybe they turned to other girls for the warmth, the passion she denied them.

But it might also be that she had never yet met anyone who "turned her on" she reminded herself. Perhaps one day she would meet a man, and know that he was the one for her just as her mother had done.

"I loved him from the first moment that I saw him," Maria had told her once, her mouth curving in tender reminiscence. "He was sitting on the hillside above the village, painting the view, in the heat of the day without even a hat to protect him from the fierceness of the sun, and I said to him, 'Why do you not sit in the shade. The sun will make you ill.' And he turned and smiled at me.''

The young artist had taken her advice, she went on, and from then on she had gone each afternoon to watch the progress of the painting.

"One day I was late, so late, because Thia Irini had made me help with some sewing. When I got to the place he was not painting at all, and when he saw me, he jumped up and said, 'I was so afraid you weren't coming and that I wouldn't see you again.' And then I knew that he loved me, also. But I had known first," Maria concluded with a look of smiling satisfaction.

How nice to have such certainty, Helen thought, particularly in view of what was to come later.

The news that Maria was to become betrothed to the son of a business acquaintance, a young man only a few years older than her seventeen-year-old self, had burst on the lovers like a bombshell.

Maria had protested to her father that she had never met the young man, but her father's attitude was inflexible. There would be plenty of opportunities for them to meet, he said. Of course, if they disliked each other, the marriage would not take place. But Maria knew there would be few grounds for dislike. Her father's choice would not have fallen on someone unsuitable, and she knew that unless she acted fast, the most subtle but inexorable pressure would be exerted and she would find herself a married woman. She knew, too, that it would be pointless to plead that she had already fallen in love with Hugo Brandon. Her father would either dismiss her plea as a young girl's fancy, or more probably, become very angry.

To his credit Hugo had been quite prepared to face Michael Korialis and endure his wrath. But Maria knew her father, and how vengeful he could be, and she persuaded Hugo that the risk would be too great. Time, too, was growing short. A big party was being planned to celebrate her betrothal, and the hour was approaching when Maria would have to meet her intended husband for the first time.

"I cannot see him. I cannot face him," she had sobbed to Hugo. "How can I greet another man, let him touch me, when it is you that I love?"

Two nights later she had left her father's house forever, leaving a note imploring his forgiveness. She had never heard another word from him as long as she lived.

Helen tried to imagine herself abandoning Hugo without a backward glance for Christopher or any of the men who had occupied her attention, however briefly. It was a ridiculous thought, she decided scornfully.

And she was enjoying life. She liked her work, and there was very little to disturb her—with the exception of her grandfather's letter, which had been disposed of, she thought with satisfaction.

A little of his own medicine, she told herself as she dried her hands and hung up the tea towel before going down to the gallery to start her day's work. And that's the end of it.

Nor was there any premonition—any pricking of her thumbs—to warn her that it was only the beginning.

THE GALLERY had the tired slightly rumpled look it always had after the opening of an exhibition, especially a successful one as that day's had been, Helen thought.

She moved around, a slim figure in her cream linen dress, straightening chairs, picking up the occasional cigarette butt that had escaped an overflowing ashtray, and returning glasses to the trays that the catering firm would pick up presently.

It had been a good day, she thought, staring around at the numerous red "sold" stickers on the paintings and pieces of sculpture on display. Paul Everard, who had stayed away from the gallery for his usual preexhibition nervous breakdown, would undergo an instant revival when he saw them, she told herself smilingly. He might even be persuaded to start painting again, if anyone could only convince him there was a permanent and enthusiastic demand for his work—which there was. She sighed a little. So many of the successful artists they handled seemed to suffer from these doubts. The failures, who came to Hugo demanding that their work be given notice, status, respect, seemed to have no such misgivings. And that, she supposed, was life.

She gave a final glance around as she prepared to depart, and frowned. One of the paintings was hanging a little askew, and that was a thing she could not endure. She went over and stood on tiptoe trying to straighten it, but only succeeded in making matters worse. There was a small stepladder in the office, but fetching it seemed too much trouble after a long and tiring day. Besides, Hugo was in the office working on the accounts and she did not want to disturb him.

She dragged forward one of the small velvet-covered chairs that were dotted around the gallery. It was fragile, but it should support her weight for the moment or two that was all she would need.

She adjusted the picture to her satisfaction, and leaned back a little to make sure it was exactly level again. The shift of her weight caused the chair to rock on its narrow legs, and she knew with a sudden shock that it was going to fall over and that she would fall with it.

She gave a little breathless cry, and in the same moment felt a pair of strong arms go around her and lift her clear. She was briefly aware of the scent of some expensive cologne and the faint aroma of cigars before she was set safely down, and turned to thank her unexpected rescuer.

Very unexpected, she thought at once, her brows lifting unconsciously as she registered him fully. Tall, but not overpoweringly so, with broad shoulders and a muscular chest, tapering down to lean hips and long legs, with a rugged strength about him that no amount of expensive tailoring could conceal. His suit was silky, light-weight and foreign looking, but then he was clearly not English himself. He was too dark, and his skin was too swarthy for that. Not a conventionally handsome face either, but one that with its strongly marked features and dark heavy-lidded eyes would not be easily forgotten. A faint smile played around the man's firm lips as he watched her watching him, she realized with sudden dismay, and felt herself blush.

She said hurriedly, "I have to thank you, *monsieur.* You saved me from a nasty accident."

"The pleasure was mine, believe me, Miss Brandon." There was a faint trace of an accent in the deep voice, but it certainly wasn't French. In fact she didn't know what it was.

She was moved by a sudden inexplicable uneasiness. She hadn't seen him in the gallery before. In fact she would have sworn he hadn't been at the exhibition at all. He was not the kind of man to be overlooked, even in a crowd. And he knew her name.

She said rather primly, "I'm afraid the gallery is closed for the day. Didn't they tell you so downstairs?"

"I didn't come to look at pictures, Miss Brandon, good as many of these are. I came to look at you."

A strange stillness seemed to encompass her.

She said carefully, suddenly thankful that Hugo was within earshot, "I'm afraid I don't understand. Do you—know me? I don't think we've met before."

"Never—until this moment," he said. "But I have seen pictures of your mother when she was a girl and you are very like her."

Her voice sharpened. "What do you want? What are you doing here? Who are you?"

"Such a lot of questions." There was faint mockery in his voice. I'll start with the last. My name is Damon Leandros, and I am here, quite simply, to persuade you to return to Greece with me to visit your grandfather."

"He sent you?" She was rigid with disbelief, then she managed a short laugh. "And what role do you fulfill in his exclusive little setup—one of the heavy mob?"

The words uttered, she wondered almost hysterically what Hugo would have said if he could have heard her being so abysmally rude to a stranger. It was out of character to say the least, and her only excuse could be this sudden inexplicable nervousness the presence of this man was engendering in her. *But why should I be nervous,* she demanded inwardly, *he can hardly kidnap me bodily.*

His eyes narrowed slightly, indicating that her words had got to him, but his tone was light as he said, "As I told you, my role is that of persuader. If I was what you imagine, I would threaten—perhaps even use force— but that's not my way."

"I suppose I must be thankful for small mercies." Helen resisted an impulse to step away from him. "But you're wasting your time, Mr. Leandros."

"You read your grandfather's letter?"

"Of course."

"Yet you did not reply to it."

"As you seem to be aware of most of the family secrets—no I didn't. Mr. Korialis should recognize the technique. He employed it often enough with my mother's letters to him."

He sighed faintly. "He was afraid that would be the reason for this silence. Would it make any difference to you to know that he regrets his treatment of your mother?"

"None at all," she said tightly. "Now we really are waiting to close for the day, so I'd be glad if you would leave."

"I'll leave when you do," he said quite equably. He hitched forward one of the velvet-covered chairs and sat down.

"I can have you thrown out, you know," she said, faltering a little at the thought of Arthur, their faithful doorman, well past his prime, being called on to deal with this muscular Greek who looked at the peak of his virility.

He tutted, his faint smile widening. "Using *your* heavy mob, Miss Brandon? But why, when I've said I intend no strong-arm tactics against you?"

She shrugged, feeling rather foolish, as she guessed he intended. "Because I've no intention of waiting here all night while you exercise your powers of persuasion, Mr. Leandros."

"Nor do I intend to spend the night here. I'd hoped you might have dinner with me."

"I'm having dinner with my father," she said. "We're very close. You might tell your *client* that."

"My 'client' also had a daughter to whom he believed he was very close," Damon Leandros said calmly. "Circumstances can change."

"And yet he let her die without a word from him," she said bitterly.

"He didn't know she was dying, and when he received the news of her death, he mourned in his heart every day that followed."

"He could have written to my father—made some move."

"You don't understand about pride? Strange," he looked at her reflectively. "I would have said you had a strong streak of it yourself."

"Let's not get into personalities, Mr. Leandros. I'm

sorry if I've been rude, but really your coming here has been a complete and utter waste of time, both yours and mine." She hesitated. "You can give Mr. Korialis my best wishes, if you want."

"Give them to him yourself."

"No." Her exasperation rose. "No, it's quite impossible. Now will you please go?"

"Helen?" In her agitation she hadn't heard the office door open and Hugo approach. Now he was standing beside them, a worried frown creasing his brow. "May I ask what's going on."

"I'm sure Mr. Leandros will be delighted to explain his errand in person," she snapped. "I've heard enough. I'm going up to the apartment."

She turned and walked away, followed by Damon Leandros's soft chuckle. She flushed, and her nails dug into the palms of her hands. He didn't seem to be taking his task very seriously, either that or he wasn't taking her very seriously. Perhaps he thought her reluctance was pretense. Well, he would learn his mistake.

Safely in the apartment, she stood for a moment making herself calm down before she continued the preparations for the evening meal that Mrs. Gibson, who acted as a nonresident housekeeper for them, had begun. The casserole of chicken and mushrooms was simmering gently in the bottom of the oven, and a lemon-meringue pie, one of her father's favorites, was standing crisp and golden brown on the counter. Helen began measuring rice into a saucepan, exclaiming in dismay when she realized she had used too much.

"Concentrate," she adjured herself fiercely. She wondered what her father was doing. Surely it couldn't be taking him all this time to get rid of their unwanted visitor? She breathed a sigh of relief as she heard the apartment door open at last, and her father call, "Helen?"

"I'm in the kitchen." She returned. She added water to the pan of rice. "Has he gone at last. He seemed very determined."

"Oh, he is."

The sardonic voice behind her made her whirl around, the color draining from her face as she registered Damon Leandros leaning negligently in the kitchen doorway watching her.

"How did you get in here?" she demanded in swift alarm. "My father...."

"Dead and his body buried under the thirteenth stair," he said in studiedly sepulchral tones, then burst out laughing. "You are wasted working in an art gallery, Miss Brandon. Such an imagination could be put to good use writing thrillers. Your father is pouring me a drink. I have been sent to inquire if you would like one also. Is everything clear to you now?"

"Like hell it is," she said furiously. She banged down the saucepan and marched to the door. She expected him to move to one side to give her passage, but he remained exactly where he was and she was forced to brush past him. A fleeting contact, but one that she would have given much to avoid.

Hugo who was busying himself with bottles and glasses, gave her a slightly apologetic look. "Dinner will stretch to three, won't it, darling?" he asked.

"It could probably feed four or five," she said in a stifled voice. "Aren't there any other strangers we could pick off the streets?"

"Helen," there was a real sharpness in her father's voice. He said, "I must apologize, Mr. Leandros, for my daughter's bad behavior. I can assure you that she isn't usually like this."

"The situation isn't very usual, either," Helen burst out. She was trembling violently and very close to tears.

"Perhaps it would be better if I went," Damon Leandros suggested. "We can always defer this discussion to a more suitable occasion."

"It won't make the slightest difference—"

"Helen," her father interposed again. "You could at least listen to what Mr. Leandros has to say. I thought perhaps in a relaxed atmosphere, over a meal in your own home you might be more willing to listen to reason."

Helen drew a shaky breath. "You—really think I ought to do as my grandfather wants and go to Greece, don't you?"

"Yes," Hugo Brandon said baldly. "I see no point in continuing a hostility that has done nothing but harm in the past. You have his blood in your veins, my dear, whether you wish to admit it or not. I suspect you also have a certain amount of curiosity about this unknown part of your family."

Desolation struck at her as she stood there between the two of them. That was something she could not deny, but she could have sworn that it was her secret and always had been. Of course she'd been curious. She could remember all the stories her mother had told her—when she was quite tiny—of life on Phoros and in the big villa that Michael Korialis owned on the outskirts of Athens. She wouldn't have been human, Helen thought, if in spite of everything she had not sometimes wondered—speculated—about all the things her mother had told her. But she had never said a word or given a hint of this to her father because she was afraid that he might be hurt, or worse, think perhaps she was hankering after the material comforts that life in a Greek millionaire's household could provide her with.

She said wearily, "I'll go and see to the dinner. I—I can't think straight."

It wasn't the most successful meal of all time. Helen could only pick at her own food, and Hugo did little better, his eyes fixed anxiously on her bent head. Only Damon Leandros seemed to have any appetite, and the ability to keep a normal conversation going, choosing safely impersonal topics.

She supposed the real discussion would take place over the coffee. She'd been aware all through dinner that Damon Leandros had been watching her, not with the concerned protectiveness of her father, but rather, she thought, as a cat might watch a mouse. She could feel resentment building up in her at his scrutiny, but she controlled it. Perhaps he was also curious about his employer's long-lost granddaughter, she thought.

One thing was certain. Michael Korialis must rely on him highly to entrust him with such an errand. She found herself wondering exactly in what capacity he worked for her grandfather, how old he was, even if he was married, then checked herself hurriedly. This kind of speculation was totally valueless.

Hugo and Damon Leandros were sitting talking while the stereo unit in the corner murmured Brahms in the background when she returned with the coffee. She set down the tray on the table, wondering if anyone would believe her if she pleaded a headache and went to her room. Then Damon Leandros bent forward to pick up his cup, and she caught the derisive smile twisting his lips as he looked at her, and she knew that he was just waiting for her to make some such excuse. Angry color rose in her cheeks. She took her own cup and retired with it stonily to the far corner of the room on the pretext that she wished to listen more closely to the music. But her seclusion was short-lived.

It was Hugo who rose with the excuse. He had run out of the small cigars he smoked and would have to go to the corner store to buy some more, he explained. He wouldn't be long, he added with a deprecatory look at his daughter.

When the door had closed behind him, she sat rigidly in her chair, staring unseeingly ahead of her, feeling the tension build in the room. There was not a word or a movement from her companion, yet she was convinced her father had simply invented the tale of needing more cigars in order to leave them alone together.

At last she stole a glance at him under her lashes, and was disconcerted to see that he was leaning back in his chair, watching her, very much at his ease.

"Relax, Miss Brandon," he said dryly. "You look as if you would splinter into a thousand pieces at the lightest touch." He saw her swallow and smiled rather grimly. "Don't be alarmed. I do not propose to test the truth of my observations."

"I should hope not." Helen found her voice. "I wouldn't think Mr. Korialis would be too pleased to know that one of his henchmen had been—mauling a member of his family."

His face was sardonic. "But as you do not propose to accompany me to Greece, there would be little chance of your grandfather ever finding out. Perhaps I should make love to you, if it means you will contact him, even if it is only to protest at my behavior."

He got up from the chesterfield and walked toward her. Helen felt herself shrinking back against the cushions.

She said huskily, "Don't you dare to touch me. Don't come near me."

He halted about a foot from her chair. Staring up at him dazedly, she thought that he seemed to tower over her.

He said softly, "You're a stubborn little fool, Eleni. What am I asking for, after all? A few weeks of your life, no more. A few weeks to give some happiness to a sick old man, holding onto his life in the hope of seeing you."

"A sick autocrat," she said bitterly. "Who has never had his slightest wish disregarded before. That was clear from the tone of his letter."

"If it were so," he said, "then you would never have been born. As for the letter, it is true that Michalis finds it difficult to ask. Is there no pity for him—no warmth under the English ice?"

"You have absolutely no right to talk to me like that." She wished desperately that he would move away. "And my name is Helen, not Eleni."

"To your grandfather, you have always been Eleni," he said quite gently, and to her horror, she felt sudden tears pricking at the back of her eyelids.

"Damn you," she whispered, then his dark face blurred, and she buried her face in her hands. When she had regained sufficient control over herself to become aware of her surroundings again, she found that he had moved away to the fireplace and was standing with one arm resting on the mantel piece, staring down at the floor. An immaculate linen handkerchief was lying on the arm of her chair, and after a brief hesitation, she used it with a muffled word of thanks.

He said, "I won't wait for your father's return." He reached into an inside pocket and produced a small leather-covered notebook and a gold pencil and wrote something before tearing off the page and putting it on the mantel piece. "My hotel and room number, Eleni," he said. "I shall be returning to Greece at the end of the week. If you wish to come with me, you have only to contact me." He paused. "Or leave a message, if you would prefer."

"I would prefer," she said tightly. "Very much I'd prefer it."

He gave her an unsmiling look. "I'm sorry we had to meet under these circumstances."

"I'm sorry we had to meet at all," she said wearily.

"But I suppose my grandfather will be grateful to you. How will you describe your victory to him, I wonder? As a knockout in the first round? Perhaps he'll give you a bonus."

He looked faintly amused. "I would hardly describe this as a victory. More in the nature of a preliminary skirmish," he said coolly. "As for my bonus—" he smiled "—I think I'll collect that now."

Two long strides brought him back to her, his hand reaching down to close like a vise on her wrist, jerking her upward. Taken off her guard, she found herself on her feet somehow, overbalancing against him, and for the second time she experienced the strength of his arms as they held her, drawing her closer still.

She said on a little gasp, "No!" And then his mouth closed on hers with merciless thoroughness.

When it was over she stood staring at him, her eyes enormous in her tear-stained face, one hand pressed convulsively against the bruised softness of her lips, too shocked to utter a word of protest.

He gave her a last cool look and turned to go. As he reached the door, Helen found her voice at last.

"You swine." She was trembling violently. "I'll make you sorry you did that."

He turned and looked back at her. "You are too late, Eleni. I am already sorry," he said, and went out.

CHAPTER TWO

HELEN UNFASTENED the shutters of her hotel room and stepped out onto the balcony, into the full force of the Athenian sun. The muted roar of the city came up from the square below as she stared around her in fascination. She had been told to rest for a few hours to prepare for the continuation of the journey to Phoros, but she could not simply lie down on her bed and forget that all Athens was spread out at her feet.

Besides she wasn't in the least tired. It had probably been the least troublesome journey she had ever undertaken, she thought. She had expected to travel on the normal scheduled flight, so the private jet had been a shock, but a pleasant one.

"This surely doesn't belong to my grandfather?" she'd asked Damon Leandros, having to forgo her fierce private intention to speak only when spoken to by him, and then only in monosyllables.

"No. It belongs to a friend of his," he said laconically. He didn't volunteer any further information on the subject, and she was determined not to ask.

The formalities at the airport were soon concluded, and a chauffeur-driven car was waiting to take them into the city. Helen had assumed she would be staying at her grandfather's villa, the one her mother had described, and she was a little surprised to be taken straight to a hotel instead, albeit a luxurious one. But it soon became clear that this was one of the hotels owned by her grandfather, a fact emphasized by the flattering welcome afforded her by the smiling manager, and the flowers and fruit that awaited her in her suite. A discreet fuss was being made, and Helen would not have been human if she had not enjoyed it.

It made up, she told herself, for having to spend the journey in Damon Leandros's company. She had not seen him from the evening he had dined at the apartment until the time the car had come to pick her up to take her to the airport.

Even when she had finally nerved herself to phone his hotel and announce that she was prepared to return to Greece with him after all, he had not been there and she'd had to leave a message with some unknown female with a husky seductive voice. Typical, Helen had thought scornfully as she replaced her receiver. The degrading way in which he had treated her had shown that Damon Leandros was the sort of man who would constantly need to be proving his virility by having some unfortunate woman in tow. She had nothing but contempt for him. It had annoyed her, too, to see the amount of deference with which he had been treated at the airport, both in Athens and back in England, while the hotel manager's greeting when they arrived had been almost servile. He was not just an ordinary employee, she decided, he must be quite big in her grandfather's organization. Well, the bigger they were, the harder they fell, she thought with satisfaction, and she could not believe that Michael Korialis would be too pleased to learn that even a trusted employee had been pawing his granddaughter.

Even though the last thing she wanted to do was spend any more time with him, nevertheless it had annoyed her when he had casually remarked that she would need a rest before the resumption of their journey, and that her lunch would be brought up to her suite.

On their way to the elevators they had passed the open doors of the dining room where a mouth-watering cold buffet was being set out, and Helen would have much preferred to have come down to the dining room and chosen a meal for herself with the rest of the guests.

Not that anyone could have complained about the selection that had been brought to her, she admitted. There had been a variety of delicious salads, cold meats, stuffed tomatoes and peppers, and a half bottle of white wine, just dry enough to suit her palate.

She had sampled everything eagerly, but if she was honest, she was too excited and too nervous to eat, and sitting on her own in a hotel room, however luxurious, was not improving the condition. She needed something to take her mind off the journey ahead of her, and the stern old man waiting for her at the end of it.

She still did not really understand why she was here. She hadn't wanted to come, and now that she was here she was beginning to realize just how alien her new environment was. People said that these days foreign capitals were growing so much alike that anyone dropped into one blindfolded would be hard put to it to decide where he was. They would never be able to say that with Athens, she thought. Even on the journey in from the airport she had realized it had an atmosphere all its own, and the glimpse she had caught of the mighty Acropolis had been breathtaking.

She glanced at her watch, which she had remembered to alter to local time. She had several hours to kick her heels in before they set off again. Surely she had time to do a little sight-seeing.

She slipped on a pair of low-heeled sandals, and reached for her bag. She had bought some travelers' checks in London and changed a few pounds into drachmas. It wasn't a great deal, but it would be enough to pay her bus fare up to the Acropolis and maybe buy her a coffee and a pastry at one of the sidewalk cafés she had noticed on her way to the hotel.

She slipped on a pair of sunglasses as she went down in the elevator. Not that she really believed anyone would try to stop her if they saw her leaving, she told herself, but Damon Leandros had been very positive about her resting in the heat of the day, and perhaps the hotel staff might feel that his orders should be reinforced.

The foyer was full of people as she stepped out of the elevator. She walked past the reception area without being observed by anyone, and out through the enormous swing doors into the sunlight.

After the air conditioning of the hotel, the heat outside struck her like a blow. She stopped at one of the newsstands and bought an English guidebook, and walked along slowly reading it. She didn't feel conspicuous in the slightest. Every second person she saw seemed to be a tourist, and no one seemed to be in a hurry. Using the map in her book, she managed to find her way to Omonia Square, and there she hesitated, finally plucking up courage to ask a passerby where she could catch a bus for the Acropolis. He gave her a wide smile, then launched into a flood of Greek interspersed with a few words of very broken English before seizing her guidebook from her hand and writing down the numbers of several buses across the top of the page. She was about to thank him and turn away when another man standing nearby decided to take a hand. Waving a peremptory finger, he seized the stub of pencil the other had been using and began to write a list of alternative numbers, beaming at Helen occasionally while his conversation with the first man became more and more heated.

Helen, aware of the curious glances of some of the passersby, was becoming embarrassed by the raised voices and violent gestures. She tried to interrupt, but the two Greeks were by now far more interested in their argument than anything else. After standing there rather helplessly for a moment, she decided to try and find the way to the nearest bus stop by herself.

Next time she wanted to know anything, she vowed silently, she would ask a policeman.

The heat was becoming oppressive now, and she was beginning to wish she had taken Damon Leandros's advice and stayed in her suite with the shutters closed. Perhaps if it had been offered as advice and less as an order, she might have felt more inclined to accept it, she told herself in self-justification. It was galling to be issued with instructions as if she was a child who could not be trusted to think for herself.

There seemed to be a great many buses around, but none of them seemed to bear any of the numbers she had been given, she realized ruefully as she stared around her. Nor were there any policemen in the vicinity.

At last in desperation she entered the nearest shop, a pharmacy, and this time she was luckier. The pharmacist, a dark young man with a beard, spoke almost perfect English, but he looked at her dubiously when she explained where she wanted to go.

"In the heat of the day, *thespinís*. Is it wise?"

"I only have a few hours in Athens," she explained.

He shrugged, looking at her slender arms revealed by the sleeveless navy dress she was wearing. "You have a very fair skin. It needs protection in our sun." He reached to one of the shelves behind him and produced a tube of sun cream. "This will help a little, but you must take care or you will burn, and that is not pleasant."

She thanked him rather doubtfully. After all, she'd only come in to find out where the bus stop was, not to spend any of her small hoard of drachmas on expensive sun cream, but when she produced her money, he waved it away.

"I do not wish payment, *thespinís*. It is my pleasure to do this for you." He smiled into her eyes with a frank sensual appreciation that sent the color racing into her face. "Perhaps one day you will come back to Athens."

He escorted her to the pavement, and pointed out to her exactly where she could catch her bus. It occurred to Helen as she moved away that with very little encouragement he would probably have come with her. And she recalled, too, that Greek women were supposed to lead quite sheltered lives until their marriage. Judging by the way the men behaved on the slightest acquaintance, they had good reason to be sheltered, she thought with faint amusement.

There were already several people waiting at the stop when she arrived, and she hoped it was a good sign and that the bus would be along very shortly. Time was passing more rapidly than she could have believed possible, and she had no idea how long the journey to the Acropolis would take.

But twenty minutes later they were still waiting, and Helen was ready to scream with frustration. Most of the the other would-be passengers had moved back from the bus stop to find themselves patches of shade, but Helen remained at the edge of the pavement, straining her eyes as she peered down the hill at the oncoming traffic.

She noticed the car at once because of its opulence and sleek lines. And then she saw who was driving it, and a little gasp escaped her. It was Damon Leandros, and he was not alone. There was a girl with him, dark and in her way as opulently beautiful as the car. She was smiling and talking to him animatedly, and at any moment the car would be past and gone. Then Damon Leandros turned slightly to flick his cigarette out of the window, and his eyes met Helen's across two

lanes of traffic. She was thankful those two lanes existed, because as well as recognition and disbelief, she had
seen the beginnings of anger in his face.

She glanced down the hill again, biting her lip
anxiously. He was caught in the traffic, and couldn't
stop, and anyway this was a one-way street. Yet
something told her that he would be back.

A battered gray taxi swerved into the side of the road
to discharge its passenger, and Helen leaped for the
opening door, almost knocking over the indignant
Athenian who emerged in her haste.

The driver was very dark and unshaven, and looked
like a member of the Greek Mafia, but he seemed to
understand that she wished to be driven to the Acropolis, even if he displayed no real inclination to take her
there. He put the car into gear with a gut-wrenching
screech, and hurled it into the stream of traffic, muttering all the time under his breath as he did so.

Helen, being bounced around in the backseat from
one side of the car to the other, was almost numb with
rage. Quite a few of the taxis she had noticed in the
streets had had the same battered look, with bumps and
dents, and sometimes even their headlights taped up,
and if this was a sample of the way they were usually
driven she could quite understand why. She wished very
much that she spoke Greek, because she doubted
whether the conventional phrase books would provide a
translation for, "Please stop driving like a maniac."

Her only consolation was that when Damon Leandros
returned to look for her, and she had not the slightest
doubt that he would, she would have vanished, hopefully without trace.

The taxi stopped at last with a jerk that almost hurled
her onto the floor, and she stared doubtfully at the mass
of figures on the meter, wondering which one depicted
the fare. The driver didn't seem prepared to help. As she

hesitated he directed a sullen stare at her, and eventually she produced her purse, peeled off a number of notes and handed them to him. Judging by the slightly contemptuous smile he gave her as he pocketed them, she had given him far too much, she thought angrily as she got out of the car.

It was hotter than ever as she walked up the hill that led to the entrance, but near the parking lot was a large stall selling cold drinks and other refreshments. There were people everywhere, sitting under the shade of the trees as they ate and drank, most of them tourists, a lot of them students propping themselves up on their bulging rucksacks. There were all sorts of accents, and Helen found she was eagerly listening for an English voice as she made her way up the slope to the summit. She would have her cold drink later, she thought, because something told her that if she ever settled under the trees, her sight-seeing would be over for the day.

The stone slabs she was walking up were warm through the thin soles of her sandals, and above her the rock towered away, crowned by a cluster of buildings. She stood there for a moment, staring up, conscious of an isolation that went deeper than mere physical loneliness. Overcome by the thought of time, and the generations of feet that had trodden this way before her—tyrants, philosophers, soldiers, slaves and conquerors—suddenly aware as she had never been of her mother's Greek blood in her veins, and of a faint stirring deep inside her that went further than the ordinary excitement of the holidaymaker.

Following the small knots of people ahead of her she made her way without haste through the propylaea and out onto the vast expanse of bleached white rock that had served the city of Athens as a fortress and a religious sanctuary. The Parthenon dominated, as she supposed it had always been intended it should. Its great honey-colored mass seemed to rear into the flawless blue of the sky, like some proud ancient lion scenting the air, Helen thought, and smiled at her own fancy.

She became aware that a group of people behind her were patiently waiting to take a photograph and stepped out of the way with a murmured word of apology. She knew that because of the wear and tear of the centuries, and more recently air pollution from the great city that circled the foot of the Acropolis, the most she could do was look and admire from a distance. Some of the buildings, she noticed glancing around her, were already supported by scaffolding. It was a shame, but at least the authorities were doing their best to preserve them for further generations of feet to tread up the long winding route from the foot of the rock

She sat down on a piece of fallen masonry, and filled her mind with images to carry away with her, because she doubted whether she would ever come back. She had agreed to undertake this journey of reconciliation because her grandfather was elderly and ill. It seemed quite likely that he was at death's door, she thought somberly, and once he was dead there would be no reason for her to return to Greece ever again. That feeling of fellowship with the past, of homecoming even that she had experienced earlier had disturbed her. She didn't understand herself. She had always regarded herself as English through and through, and wholly her father's daughter. She had never looked Greek, she thought in perplexity.

After a while she rose and walked to the edge, threading her way between the chattering groups with their clicking cameras. The view was stupendous. She thought she could even catch a glimpse of the sea in the distance.

She turned away at last, feeling a little giddy. The sun reflecting off the white rock she stood on was almost overwhelming, like some exotic moonscape. It would surely be cooler, more bearable indoors. She went down a brief flight of steps, past a large stone owl and into the museum. She found an unoccupied bench and sank down onto it, pressing her fingers against her forehead with a little sigh.

When the hand descended on her shoulder she looked up with a start, thinking it was one of the attendants. Instead she found herself looking into the coldly furious face of Damon Leandros.

"Oh." She stared up at him, her brows drawing together. "It's you. How did you find me?"

"It did not require a great deal of thought to deduce where you were going," he said icily. "I saw you enter the museum and followed. What is the matter? Are you ill?"

"A slight headache, that's all," she returned stiffly and heard his exasperated sigh.

"I asked you to rest for precisely this reason," he said after a pause. "I do not wish to present you to your grandfather suffering from heatstroke or exhaustion."

"Of course not, although I needn't ask whether that's prompted by concern for me or concern for your job." She pushed her hair back from her face with defiant fingers. "I suppose my grandfather might not be too pleased that you'd left me to my own devices."

He gave her a long hard look. "Your grandfather was perfectly well aware that I had business to attend to this afternoon, and that our departure for Phoros would be delayed for a few hours."

"Really?" Helen smiled in spite of her pounding head. "I saw your 'business' beside you in the car. Nice work if you can get it," she added with deliberately airy vulgarity.

But the expected explosion did not transpire. When he did speak his voice was softer than ever.

"Miss Brandon, did your father never beat you when you were a child?"

"Of course not." Helen dismissed from her mind the memory of numerous childish chastisements. "Why do you ask?"

"Idle curiosity. There could, of course, be no other reason." His tone was silky. "Are you prepared to return to the hotel with me now and rest?"

Helen lifted her chin. "But I haven't had a chance to look around the museum yet," she objected.

"Then by all means let us do so." She didn't like the smile he gave her as he lifted her to her feet.

Half an hour later she was wishing with all her heart that she had meekly acceded to his original suggestion of returning to the hotel. Her head was pounding almost intolerably, and she felt desperately thirsty and slightly queasy at the same time. At any other time—and of course if he'd been anyone else—she would have been fascinated by what he was telling her about the transition from the archaic to the classical style in sculpture, but his words seemed to buzz meaninglessly in her ears. And the curving smiles on the Korai, the maidens carved out of stone as offerings to the virgin goddess of the city, Athena, seemed to mock her everywhere she looked.

She swallowed, staring down at the floor, refusing to admit defeat. She was being a fool, she knew. After all, he had been detailed by her grandfather to look after her, and she was sure she only had to give a hint and she would be out of this increasingly stuffy atmosphere and back in that comfortable hotel room with the shutters closed. But if she asked him to take her back, he would have won in some obscure way and that she could not allow. She gave a little stifled sigh, and forced herself to concentrate on the head of a boy known as the "blond youth," Damon told her, because there were still traces of yellow tint found on it when it was discovered.

"We have always admired blond hair, you see." Her companion's voice sounded amused. "On Phoros, near your grandfather's villa, there is a ruined temple that archaeologists say was dedicated to Aphrodite. She is usually pictured as having blond hair, too."

Helen said faintly, "She could be bald as a coot for me. I—I really must get out of here. I can't breathe."

The events of the next hour or so were mercifully blurred. Later she would remember details like the strength of his arm around her, and the way the cushions of that sleek car of his seemed to support her like a cloud. As they drove back to the hotel she found herself wondering, as she tried to control the waves of threatened nausea, what he had done with the dark beauty she had seen him with, but inquiring was altogether too much trouble. Besides, she tried to tell herself, what did it matter how many women he had?

She could remember vomiting tiredly until her throat and her stomach ached, and how the tiled bathroom swung in a dizzying arc around her, and the refreshing sensation of a towel dipped in cold water wiping her face, and being placed across her forehead as at last—at long last—she lay down on the bed and closed her eyes.

When she opened them again it was early evening, judging by the length of the shadows across the floor. She sat up gingerly. Her head still ached, but she no longer felt that terrible debilitating nausea. In fact she was almost hungry. She pushed back the single sheet that was the only covering provided on the bed, and started to get out, catching as she did so, an astonished glimpse of herself in the long mirror opposite. She looked a mess, she thought candidly. Her eyes looked twice their normal size and her hair hung on her shoulders in a tangle, but that was incidental. All she was wearing was her underclothes, a dark blue lace bra and matching brief panties. Her navy dress was hanging over the back of a chair with her sandals placed neatly beside it, and she couldn't for the life of her remember removing any of them.

She got up and went over to the dressing table, reaching for her hairbrush that had been among the small amount of hand luggage she had unpacked, and starting to smooth her hair into its usual face-curving style. She looked wan, she thought critically, but cosmetics would soon improve that. She wandered into the bathroom and had a long leisurely wash, spraying herself liberally with L'air du temps when she had finished.

She would phone down for some soup, she thought, and also inquire if there were any messages for her. It was already well past the time that Damon Leandros had proposed they should set off for Phoros, and she supposed he would be waiting somewhere. Grudgingly she had to admit that he had been kind enough during the dash back to the hotel, and that he had at least left her alone to recover from her sickness.

She sauntered back into the bedroom, and stopped dead, her eyes widening in disbelief. Damon Leandros was there, lounging nonchalantly against the long row of built-in closets that filled one wall. For a moment their gazes locked, and then his eyebrows rose mockingly and she remembered too late that she was half naked.

She looked around wildly for her dress, but he was between her and the chair on which it lay. As if he guessed what was going through her mind, he turned and reached for it, tossing it to her. She snatched at it thankfully, and dragged it over her head, her hands fumbling as she sought to reach and close the long back zipper.

He watched her efforts for a moment or two, a derisive smile curling his lips, then he moved toward her and she took an instinctive step backward.

"Relax," he advised curtly. "I have no intention of raping you, but you seem to need help."

"I don't need anything from you," Helen choked, still struggling ineffectually with the damned zipper.

"You didn't say that a few hours ago while I was holding your head in the bathroom," he said. "Besides, I may have damaged the zipper when I removed the dress. I was in a hurry and they are fragile things."

Helen pressed her hands against burning cheeks. "*You*—it was *you*? Oh, how could you? How *dared* you?"

"There was no question of daring," he said coolly. "I thought English girls gloried in their liberation from outdated conventions. Besides, you were and are perfectly adequately clothed. I daresay you will wear far less when you go swimming on Phoros."

"Well, at least you won't be there to see," Helen flashed. "I doubt whether Mr. Korialis will regard your activities in quite the same liberated way."

"So you intend to make use of your Greek parentage when it suits you. I find that interesting." He walked over to her before she could retreat again and spun her around, his hands on her shoulders. Helen felt the recalcitrant zipper move upward, and for one infinitely disturbing minute the brush of his fingers strangely cool on the heated skin of her spine. She tensed involuntarily at his touch, and heard him laugh softly.

"I'm glad I amuse you," she said tersely as she pulled away from him. "I think you'll laugh on the other side of your face when you find yourself out of a job."

"You intend that your grandfather should dismiss me?" he inquired lazily.

"How right you are." She faced him defiantly, her chin up, eyes sparkling.

He shrugged. "You can always try, Eleni."

"And please don't call me that. It—it's familiar."

"Which is of course unthinkable," he said solemnly. But he was amused, and she knew he was and it infuriated her.

"How the hell did you get into my room anyway? Surely the staff wouldn't have allowed...."

"Oh, I can be very persuasive when I want. But in this case I didn't have to be. When I left after attending to your...needs I simply took your key with me." He touched his jacket pocket. "I have it here."

She held out her hand. "Give it to me, please."

"Why? You won't need it again. We are leaving soon. As it is I have had to telephone your grandfather and tell him we have been delayed." He paused. "He wasn't pleased, and it is bad for him to suffer any agitation."

"And I suppose you made haste to tell him it was all my fault," she said with heavy irony.

"I told him merely that you have been tired by your journey from England, and that the heat had affected you. I did not tell him you had been mad enough to try and explore the Acropolis in the full blaze of noon without allowing yourself to become in any way acclimatized. Michael Korialis is not one of those who—to use your English phrase—suffers fools gladly. I didn't wish you to make a bad impression immediately."

She gave him an outraged look. "The implication being that I'll make one eventually."

"I think it is inevitable. You are willful, disobedient, and have a sharp tongue. None of these are attributes to appeal to a man who adheres to the old ways like your grandfather. You have a lot to learn about Greece and its men, Eleni."

"I'd prefer to have no more lessons from you," she said baldly.

He smiled. "As you plan to have me dismissed as soon as we get to Phoros, there will be little opportunity for such lessons," he said smoothly, but his dark eyes held an odd glint, and Helen bit her lip in sudden uncertainty. Perhaps she shouldn't have clashed with him quite so openly. Her grandfather had obviously given him a great deal of power, and it had gone to his head. But it might have been better to have waited to declare her enmity until they were safely on Phoros. But she'd not been able to help herself. The thought of him looking at her, touching her when she was sick and helpless made her feel ill all over again.

She should have retaliated after he had kissed her in London, she thought vengefully as she repacked her small case. She should have hit him or scratched his face with her nails, then he would not have dared take these kind of liberties. And she ignored the small warning voice that suggested that a man like Damon Leandros took what he chose, as he wished, and without counting the cost.

As she worked she was aware of him watching her, his dark face enigmatic as she thrust her cosmetic bag on top of her night things, and threw her hairbrush in after them.

As she clicked the locks shut she ignored his outstretched hand.

"Perhaps you would bring the others." She nodded toward her other cases standing under the window.

"I'll have them brought down, certainly," he said evenly after a pause, and she suppressed a grin. Beneath his dignity, obviously, to walk behind her carrying two large cases, she thought. Perhaps she had discovered his vulnerable point. He didn't like to look ridiculous. And that, she thought, with the vaguest germ of an idea forming in her head, could be just too bad for Mr. Macho Leandros.

As she walked along the corridor toward the elevator, Helen became aware of two excitedly giggling chambermaids observing her from a linen room. She glanced questioningly at Damon, who smiled faintly.

"They are pleased to see you," he said. "Your grandfather is a much loved man."

She felt as if he was waiting for some special response from her, but she could give none. The prospect of meeting her grandfather was becoming more and more formidable.

She entered the elevator in silence and stood waiting while her companion pressed the "down" button.

"How do we get to Phoros?" she asked at last, more to break the silence than from any desire for information.

"There is a car waiting to take us to Piraeus. From there we make a journey by sea," he said laconically.

"Oh." Helen digested this. "I suppose there is a regular ferry service, even though it is only a small island?"

"It runs three times a day."

The faint wish to make him look ridiculous that had been buzzing in her mind now began to take shape.

It would give her great satisfaction, she thought, to arrive on Phoros alone, having left Damon Leandros ignominiously behind in Athens. She wished she had thought of it earlier while she was still in her room. Perhaps she could have lured him into the bathroom and locked him in somehow, although she had a feeling the only bolt had been on the inside of the door. Well, she would just have to think of something else.

As they emerged from the elevator Helen saw her remaining luggage being carried out to the car ahead of them. If this was a sample of the service provided by all her grandfather's hotels, then it could hardly be faulted, she thought wryly.

"Don't we have to check out or something," she asked a little desperately as they moved past the reception desk.

"That's all been taken care of."

"But my key," she persisted. "You've still got my key."

"I left it in the door of your room."

Oh, blast, Helen thought savagely. If she could have delayed him at reception even for a moment or two she might have been able to get out to the car and persuade the driver to leave without him.

She could hardly believe her own fortune when she heard one of the receptionists call after him, and saw him hesitate with obvious impatience before he turned back toward the desk.

"You go ahead," he directed briefly. "I hope only to be a few minutes."

"Take as long as you like," Helen sent him a dazzling smile. Her heart beating rapidly, she walked toward the door. The car, an opulent vehicle of a make that she didn't immediately recognize was at the curb, and a man in a chauffeur's uniform was standing beside it. When he saw Helen coming toward him, he threw open the rear passenger door with some ceremony.

She got in trying to appear calm and in control of the situation.

"Do you speak English?" she asked.

"Only a little, *thespinís.*"

"That's fine." She made herself speak slowly and deliberately so that he would understand. "I want to leave at once. We must go quickly to catch the ferry."

The man's face was a picture of astonishment. He started to say something about Kýrios Leandros, but Helen swiftly interrupted.

"Kýrios Leandros cannot come with us. He has been

delayed." She mimed a telephone call. "He is too busy. He will come later."

The driver gave her a long doubtful look, then stared at the hotel entrance as if willing Kýrios Leandros to appear like the Demon King and put an end to his uncertainty. But no one emerged.

"Please hurry." Helen applied a little more pressure. "If I miss the ferry, my grandfather Michael Korialis will be angry."

It was clear the Korialis name had pull with the driver, because with a fatalistic shrug, he got into the driver's seat and started the car. Helen sat back in her seat, allowing a little relieved sigh to escape her lips. She wished she could be around when Damon Leandros finished taking his phone call, or whatever he was doing, and came out of the hotel to find the car gone and her with it. But you couldn't have everything in this life, and she was more than content to be speeding toward Piraeus and the Phoros ferry without him.

And let him explain that away to my grandfather along with everything else, she thought.

The drive to Piraeus was a little disappointing as the road lay through rather dusty suburbs and industrial estates, and the scenery was flat and uninspiring. Helen found it difficult to relax. She felt exhilarated, and a little nervous at the same time, and could not resist taking brief looks back over her shoulder, as if she half expected to see Damon Leandros following them.

But that was impossible, she told herself confidently. He'd have to find another car, and that would take time. She glanced at her watch wondering what time the Phoros ferry left. The traffic was heavy, and the car was constantly being forced to slow almost to a crawling pace if not stop altogether. But recalling her experience of waiting for the bus, it occurred to Helen that timetables were obviously not as strictly adhered to in

Greece as in the rest of creation. Certainly the driver did not seem at all agitated by the frequent delays, and the easiest thing to do was to follow his example.

She sighed in relief as the harbor came in sight, and sat forward, waiting for the car to stop. But it did not stop. The driver steadily threaded his way through the other vehicles, both moving and stationary, that packed the narrow streets, narrowly avoiding laughing chattering groups of people who roamed across the crowded highway as if it was just another extension of the narrow footpath.

There seemed to be steamers everywhere, Helen thought dazedly as she stared out of the window, and hundreds of people boarding and disembarking. She only hoped the driver knew what he was doing, and that her escapade would not end in her sailing off into the wide blue yonder on the wrong ship.

She tapped the driver on the shoulder. "Which is the ferry?" she asked.

But his only response was an owlish look and a faint shrug of the shoulders as if her meaning escaped him.

"Boat. Phoros," she tried again, and this time to her relief he nodded, smiling broadly.

"Soon, soon, *thespinis*."

And with that she had to be content. The car moved on, away from the harbor and the scent of exhaust fumes mingling with the more pervasive odors of charcoal grills and olive oil, and out onto a winding road. Helen twisted around, staring at the clustering vessels they were leaving behind. She could only hope the driver knew what he was doing as they left the vast sprawl of the waterfront behind them. The road they were on seemed to have been carved out of the vast cliffs themselves, and some of the views were spectacular, she had to admit. She was intrigued, too, by the numerous little shrines and grottoes that dotted the wayside. Thanks offerings, she supposed, but to which gods—the ancient or modern? Perhaps in a country such as Greece the old pagan undercurrents still ran strong.

The road turned downhill, and she saw another smaller harbor beneath them, where sleek motor launches and small yachts lay at anchor. It looked the last place in the world where a public ferry for a small place like Phoros would leave from, and she leaned forward frowning a little.

The driver looked back at her, as if aware of her uncertainty, and pointed downward, saying something in his own tongue that was clearly intended to be reassuring. She made herself smile back, but her tension showed in her smile. She was at the end of one journey, perhaps, but at the beginning of another. And at the end of it was a man who, although unseen, had seemed to dominate her childhood and adolescence; on whose character, whose pride, arrogance and lack of compassion she had speculated so often and to so little avail. Yet soon they would meet, and her stomach churned involuntarily at the thought. If her grandfather could be judged by the caliber of the men he chose to employ... she thought, then resolutely switched her mind to other less disturbing ideas. He had sent for her, he wanted to see her, so surely that indicated a softening of his earlier implacable attitude. Or at least she had to hope so, or the few weeks she was committed to spending in Greeece could well be unendurable.

She wished she had never allowed herself to be persuaded to come to Greece, if persuasion was the word. Emotional blackmail might be more appropriate, she thought bitterly, remembering how Damon Leandros had deliberately played on her heightened sensibilities. He was to blame. He was to blame for everything.

The car drove slowly along the waterfront, past open-air cafés whose gay awnings fluttered in the slight evening breeze. There were people everywhere. Tourists tentatively sipping their first tastes of ouzo and retsina, and the usual anonymous groups of men talking, the bright strings of worry beads in their hands moving incessantly as they gestured to lend emphasis to their remarks. The main waterfront at Piraeus had almost been too crowded to assimilate, but here Helen had time to look around her and take in some of the atmosphere.

It was soon obvious the driver was no stranger here, and this in itself was a reassurance to her. The car was recognized and voices called and hands lifted in greeting, to which he responded. He drove slowly along the curve of the quayside almost to the far end before stopping. Then he turned to Helen.

"Boat here, *thespinís,*" he announced.

There certainly was a boat, but not the small rather scruffy steamer she had ruefully envisaged as the most likely craft to be plying between Piraeus and an unimportant island. It was a large impressive cruiser with cabin accommodation and what appeared to be a sun deck with an awning. And was that a radio mast, she wondered in bewilderment.

The driver had opened her door by this time and was standing patiently waiting for her to alight.

Helen gestured weakly at the cruiser. "This?" she asked with a shake of her head.

He nodded vigorously. "Phoros boat, *thespinís.* You hurry. They wait for you."

How very obliging of them, Helen thought, sudden amusement rising within her. Her suspicions about the timetable were apparently totally justified, and she would bet the other passengers were blessing her by now.

A flight of steps led down from the harbor wall, and at the bottom a man in a white uniform was waiting to help her on board. Helen waited while her luggage was speedily transferred to the cruiser, and smiled as the driver returned up the steps.

"Efcharistó," she said shyly, trying out one of the few Greek words she knew.

"Parakaló." He removed his cap. "Go with God, *thespinís."*

The cruiser had indeed been waiting for her, Helen decided, because as soon as her feet touched the deck it seemed to become a hive of discreet activity, and she could feel the throb of powerful engines springing into life. Her cases had vanished, she noticed, and she stood feeling rather solitary, and a little lost.

A man wearing jeans and a pale blue vest that showed off a powerful torso and arms went past her, and Helen detained him with a quick, "Oh, please." He paused, looking at her inquiringly.

She shrugged rather helplessly. "Where are the passengers?" she asked. "How long does it take to get to Phoros?"

He spread his hands out in front of him. *"Then sas katalavéno, thespinís."*

"You don't speak English," Helen said resignedly, and turned away, to find the man in the white uniform beside her.

"Welcome to the *Phaedra,* Miss Brandon." He said with a heavy accent. "It is pleasant on deck, *ne*? But there are refreshments below, if you prefer."

Some coffee, Helen thought longingly. The aroma emanating from the tavernas they had passed on the way here had served to remind her just how hungry she was, and how Damon Leandros had rushed her off from the hotel without allowing her to order the soup she had craved.

"I'd like to go below," she said rather shyly. She looked around the deck. "Is—are the other passengers there, too?"

"As you say, *thespinís*." He smiled with a flash of white teeth, and led her to a companionway. The passage it led to was wider than she had expected, its walls paneled in wood, and there were doors on each side. The first one they passed was open and glancing in Helen saw it was the galley. A swarthy white-coated steward was busy putting the finishing touches to what appeared to be an extensive cold buffet. If this was for the benefit of the passengers, as she supposed it must be, then it was clear no expense had been spared. It was incredible, she thought. The only explanation could be that there were two classes of ferry available to Phoros, one for the general public, and this one for the exclusive use of the privileged classes who had their holiday villas on Phoros. It all fitted in with everything that had happened to her on the journey so far—the private jet, the luxury of the hotel. There were definite advantages in being related to Michael Korialis, she thought with a certain irony, and probably that was what she was intended to think.

The officer stopped so abruptly that Helen, lost in her meditation, nearly cannoned into him. He knocked softly on a door before opening it with something of a flourish, then stood aside to give Helen access to the large saloon beyond.

Her dazed eyes took in deeply cushioned leather seating, low tables, and a well-stacked bar in one corner. And all for her benefit, because there wasn't another soul in there. She took a wondering step forward, and then from the doorway behind her the last voice in the world that she had expected or wanted to hear ever again said softly, "Welcome on board the *Phaedra,* Eleni."

CHAPTER THREE

SHE TURNED AND STARED at him, her face, her whole tense stance reflecting the shock and disbelief she was experiencing.

"You." She was almost choking. "But why—how...?"

"It is quite simple." He moved forward, shutting the saloon door behind him. Shutting the world out, she found herself thinking wildly, shutting them in alone together. "I took my own car and a different route. Did you really think I would allow you to leave me behind, and make the rest of your journey alone? Your grandfather asked me to bring you to him, and I shall do so, Eleni, whether you wish it or not."

"Well, I don't wish it," she said defiantly.

"You have already made that more than clear. But you must have realized by now that in spite of your hostility to me, I find certain compensations in your company." His eyes rested momentarily on her mouth them moved downward, slowly and deliberately as if he was mentally recreating the physical action of stripping the simple navy dress from her as he had done only a few hours earlier.

She said rather frantically, 'I think I'll go back on deck."

"And I think that you will stay here," he said quite quietly, his body a barrier between her and the door. "I warn you, Eleni, if you provoke a scene, you will make no one ridiculous except yourself. The crew will obey my orders and not yours. Now sit down. Dimitri will be bringing our meal in a few minutes.''

''Food would choke me,'' Helen declared with furious inaccuracy.

''That is unfortunate,'' he said sardonically. ''Then you may sit and watch me eat.''

She flung herself down on the long cushioned seat that ran the length of one wall of the saloon.

''I will make you sorry for this,'' she said in a low voice. ''I promise that I'll make you sorry.''

''I believe that you will try,'' he said slowly. ''It remains to be seen whether you will succeed. If you continue to deliberately provoke me, you could be the one who is sorry.''

''Are you threatening me, Mr. Leandros?''

''No, merely warning you, Miss Brandon,'' he retorted with mocking formality. She longed to hit him, to see her finger marks on that dark face, but she did not dare. She couldn't be certain what kind of reprisals he might exact, and she did not wish to find out.

There was another swift deferential knock at the door, and the steward entered, his eyes flicking curiously from one to the other. He spoke to Damon Leandros in Greek, and received a brief reply in the same language.

Helen crouched on the seat, watching sullenly as the man pulled up one of the tables and placed a chair carefully opposite where she was sitting. In a matter of moments, a spotless linen tablecloth had been added, together with cutlery, plates and wineglasses.

Damon Leandros walked over to the bar and picked up a bottle of whiskey.

''May I offer you a drink, Eleni.''

''I want nothing from you,'' she bit at him.

''If you continue to take that tone, you may get more than you bargain for,'' he said harshly. ''Dimitri speaks no English, but he is far from deaf, and you will oblige me by behaving civilly in his presence. Now, I ask you again. Would you like a drink?''

She did not look at him. ''Yes—thank you. I—I'll have a retsina,'' she added with a shade of bravado.

His brows rose and he gave her a searching look. ''Really? You would not prefer martini or campari?''

''I'd like retsina,'' she insisted stubbornly. ''I know what it's supposed to taste like, and I still would like to try it.''

He shrugged. ''As you wish.'' He poured a modest amount of pale liquid into a glass and brought it to her before settling himself in the chair opposite. She knew he was watching her intently to see her reaction as she lifted the glass to her lips, and steeled herself. As it was, even the first cautious sip caught her by the throat, and for a few seconds she was terrified that she was going to choke ignominiously. It was like drinking pure resin, she thought furiously, and she was sure he had done it deliberately because she knew there were many quite mildly resinated varieties available.

''Cheers,'' she said ironically, setting the glass down.

''*Yá sas.*'' He lifted his own glass courteously, a faint smile playing around his mouth. ''Is the retsina to your liking?''

''Perfectly,'' she lied. ''It—it's everything I've always heard about it.''

Dimitri was bustling backward and forward. She heard the subdued pop of a cork being withdrawn, and prayed that the wine was something slightly more palatable. He set a platter of crusty bread on the table, and a bowl of something that looked like mayonnaise but smelled intriguingly of garlic and other things. Helen could not restrain a slight gasp when he placed a dish of huge succulent prawns on the table between them, then withdrew from the saloon at a slight unsmiling nod from her companion. Helen was sorry to see him go. The prospect of dining *tête-á-tête* with Damon was a disturbing one. She remembered the last time she had dined in his company at the apartment in London, and the unexpected aftermath, the memory of which still had the power to tighten her nerves and make her mouth dry.

She stole an unobtrusive glance at her watch, wondering how many hours of his company she would be forced to endure before they reached Phoros. She took another sip of retsina, and found to her surprise that it improved on acquaintance. Which was more than could be said for her companion, she thought, and smiled to herself.

"You are amused about something?" He was leaning back in the chair, watching her with half-closed eyes.

"Not really." She gave a slight shrug, then leaned forward and helped herself to one of the prawns.

He pushed the bowl of dip toward her. "Would you like to try some of this?"

"I don't know," she said doubtfully. "If it has a lot of garlic. . . ."

"Don't worry." It was his turn to be amused. "I intend to have some, too."

She had taken another sip of retsina before she realized what he meant, and flushed hotly.

"You flatter yourself, Mr. Leandros."

"I think we both know that I don't," he said evenly, and his eyes went to her mouth again, his expression suddenly sensuous as if he was remembering exactly how its softness had felt under his.

Helen took another sip of her drink, and another prawn, shaking her head vehemently as he offered the dip again. He shrugged and put the bowl on another table, offering her the bread in its place with an ironic smile.

She took a piece, then steadying her voice, said in what she hoped was a normal conversational tone, "I take it that *Phaedra* is in no way part or the normal ferry service to Phoros."

"In no way," he agreed.

"So you lied to me," she said.

"In what way did I lie?"

"You let me think we would be traveling on the ferry. You knew perfectly well that I...that I wouldn't want..." her voice tailed away lamely.

"To sail off with me into the darkness of the Aegean night?" he asked smoothly. "You have only yourself to blame for that. We could have left several hours earlier and reached Phoros in daylight. And I did not lie. I mentioned only a sea journey. It was you that decided we would be traveling on the public ferry."

"That's just playing with words," she said hotly. "You should have told me what was really happening. Does—does *Phaedra* belong to my grandfather?"

"No," he said. "Are you disappointed?"

"Just curious," she said. "I suppose it belongs to another of his wealthy friends. He's lucky to have so many."

"Michael has perhaps been more fortunate in his friends than in his relations," he said dryly.

Helen went rigid, "That's an abominable thing to say." Her voice rose in anger.

"Oddly enough, I did not mean you. But are you really trying to claim that your behavior has been beyond reproach?"

"I am going to Phoros. Isn't that what everyone wants?"

"Not if you are going full of resentment, determined to rub salt into old wounds, Eleni. If you are going to your grandfather to exact some kind of personal retribution, then it would have been better if you had stayed in London."

"Now he tells me," she said savagely. "What shall I do? Swim back to Piraeus?"

"No," he said coldly. "Try and search your heart for some glimmer of the compassion I found in you that night in London."

She opened her eyes wide, staring at him over the rim of her glass.

"Oh—I *see*. It's the soft yielding bit that turns you on. That was where my last so-called glimmer of compassion led, wasn't it—to being grossly insulted by you."

"You have a gift for exaggeration," he said harshly. "Also for provocation. I would take care, Eleni."

"It's you that needs to take care," she said recklessly. "I won't forget any of it, you know. The ambiguous remarks—the degrading way you treated me this afternoon. I'm going to tell my grandfather every sordid detail."

"I see I didn't underestimate your capacity for vengeance," he drawled. "Perhaps you also underestimate me."

"I don't think so." She set down her empty glass. She felt quite light-headed, and wondered uneasily whether it was anticipation of her coming victory, or merely the effect of retsina on her still-empty stomach. She hastily ate some more bread, and helped herself again to the luscious prawns.

"I'm glad to see you have recovered from your indisposition," he said indolently after a few minutes. "Also that the color has returned to your face. You clearly enjoy the stimulation of a fight."

"I always considered until now that I was the peace-loving type," she said tartly. "I suppose you find that difficult to believe."

"A desire for peace is usually the prerogative of the elderly. Someone as young as you, Eleni, should love life and all it has to offer." He finished his whiskey. "Perhaps until now you have only been half alive."

"I've been perfectly happy," she said indignantly.

"That is impossible." Deftly he opened the wine and poured it into the waiting glasses. "Perfection in happiness is not so easily attained. You have possibly been content, but no more."

Helen tilted her chin. "May we change the subject please," she requested coldly. "I've no wish to sit here and listen to your assumptions about me."

He smiled and lifted his glass in a mocking toast to which she made no response whatever.

Dimitri appeared silently to remove their plates and serve the next course—tiny chickens, their flesh delicately flavored with herbs, and a large serving tray set with dishes of every conceivable type of salad. Fingerbowls with flower petals floating on the surface of the water were placed on the table beside them before he withdrew again as quietly as he had arrived.

It was all very impressive, but then she supposed it was intended to be. Everything that had happened was meant to underline the contrast between the modest comfort of her past circumstances, and the luxury she was to encounter in the immediate future. She felt a thrill of apprehension that deepened as she looked up and encountered the dark brooding gaze of her companion.

Her appetite seemed to have deserted her suddenly, and she only picked at the food in front of her.

"Is the meal not to your liking?"

She started as Damon Leandros's voice intruded on her thoughts.

"It's all delicious," she said hastily. "Perhaps it's just the—the motion of the boat."

His eyebrows rose and he sent her a look of cynical disbelief. She supposed it had been a foolish thing to say. The sea was so calm, it was hard to believe they were on board ship.

"You are a poor sailor?"

"I haven't done a great deal of sailing. My life has been spent in a city," she reminded him.

"Of course. You have missed a great deal."

"But none of the things that matter. All this—" she gestured around her "—is purely incidental."

"How very high-minded of you," he said with a faint smile. "You despise money and the material comforts it can provide?"

"Of course not. My father isn't exactly a poor man, you know."

"No," he said after a pause. "He seems to have done well enough for himself. It is to his credit that he has done so."

"To his credit?" she echoed.

"His life was very different when he married your mother," he said evenly.

She gasped. "You mean—you're insinuating that daddy was a fortune hunter. Oh, of course." Her voice stung. "There would have to be an ulterior motive. It wouldn't suit Greek machismo, would it, to admit that my mother preferred an Englishman to an arranged marriage with one of her own countrymen—someone she probably didn't even know. She actually dared rebel—break out of the mold, so naturally all kinds of excuses have to be made. After all, she set a dangerous precedent, didn't she. Other women might decide to take a hand in their own destinies, and that wouldn't suit the arrogant Grecian male. You did invent the word 'tyrant' didn't you?"

"Not personally." He was still smiling, but there was a flicker of anger in his eyes. "You speak very strongly,

Eleni. You who come from the permissive society where divorces can almost be bought across a counter like any other commodity. Yet you criticize us because we are concerned for our women—concerned for their comfort and security.''

"So concerned,'' she said tightly, "that when a woman sins against your male-dictated male-orientated code, she is simply cast out, as my mother was. Her letters unanswered, her whole existence ignored. Some caring. Some concern. Well, thank God she had my father.''

"I will say amen to that, at least.'' He would have said more, she knew, only at that moment the saloon door reopened and Dimitri entered. He must have sensed the tension in the air, Helen thought, because she could sense the quick questioning glance he gave them as he cleared the plates. The question soon gave way to reproach, however, when he saw how little she had eaten, muttering a few remarks in his own language for good measure.

"What does he say,'' Helen asked as Dimitri, sadly shaking his head, placed a bowl of ripe peaches and glossy purple grapes as large as damsons on the table.

"He grieves for your lack of appetite.''

"Will you tell him I'm sorry.''

"Can you not tell him yourself?''

"I can manage 'please' and 'thank you' but that's all.''

"Quite incredible,'' he said, adding more wine to his glass as Helen declined any more to drink, her hand over the top of her glass. "One would think you were determined to deny your Greek blood.''

"I've never been very conscious of it, but surely that's understandable under the circumstances.''

"It is fortunate, then, that your circumstances have changed.''

"But I haven't," Helen pointed out as Dimitri set down a huge silver coffeepot. "And I regard myself as totally English."

"A few lessons with Madame Stavros will soon change that, I think."

Helen was barely conscious of Dimitri making his soft-footed way to the door. "Who is Madame Stavros?"

"She is the widow of a friend of your grandfather's—a former diplomat. She has traveled widely with her late husband and speaks several languages fluently, including your own. Your grandfather has engaged her to be a companion for you, and to give you a basic grounding in Greek."

"But that's the most ridiculous thing I have ever heard," Helen protested. "I was invited for a few weeks' holiday, not to go back to school. And I certainly don't need a female companion. Besides, doesn't my grandfather's sister Thia Irini still live with him?"

"Kýria Atrakis speaks little English." He paused. "You will like Madame Stavros."

"Is that an opinion or an order?" Helen watched his mouth tighten ominously. "Not that it really matters. I expect I can convince my grandfather that a girl brought up in the heart of the permissive society, as you yourself mentioned, is in no need of a chaperone, however many languages she may speak." She smiled at him across the table. "Shall I pour the coffee?"

"As you wish." He pushed back his chair and rose, walking over to the bar.

The coffee was black and very strong, but Helen welcomed it, hoping it would counteract some of the effects of the retsina that were now making themselves felt. Her head was light, and her legs did not even appear to exist anymore. She'd been a fool to drink so much of it when she wasn't used to it, she berated herself mentally.

Quietly she slipped off her sandals and tucked the offending legs beneath her on the long cushioned seat while she sipped her coffee and then put down her cup.

He walked back across the saloon, glass in hand, and stood looking down at her. He looked very tall, suddenly, and she remembered that evening in the London apartment, and had to dig her nails in the palms of her hands to stop herself visibly shrinking back against the cushions.

"Shall we go up on deck?" His eyes were fixed on her face, but she could not read their expression. "The moon will have risen by now."

Helen swallowed. "I think I'd prefer to stay here. The, er, motion of the boat."

"Oh, yes, I had forgotten," he said smoothly. "Then let us by all means remain here." And to Helen's consternation he sat down beside her, so near that his thigh brushed hers. She hurriedly reached forward and picked up her coffee cup, realizing too late it was empty, and knowing that he knew it, too.

"What is the matter, Eleni? Have you suddenly realized that you are a long way from London?"

Almost casually he put one hand on her knee, pushing her skirt up toward her thigh. Cup and saucer went flying as she struck at his hand in outrage.

"How dare you," she choked.

He gave a low laugh. "Why should I not dare? You already mean to present an adverse report on my behavior to your grandfather, and you have a saying, have you not, that one might as well be hung for a sheep as a lamb. Well, then."

His other arm went around her pulling her against him without haste. She struggled wildly, her hands pushing against his chest, trying to fend him off.

"Let go of me," she raged. "Have you gone mad?"

"No," he said harshly. "Just curious about this

much vaunted permissive society of yours, Eleni. Stop fluttering, little bird, and show me how a liberated woman behaves with her man.''

Lean fingers encircled both her slender wrists, pinioning them securely, and his dark head bent until his mouth touched the hollow of her throat. She gasped with helplessness and fright, and another subtler emotion that she could neither explain nor understand.

''I—I'll scream,'' she threatened huskily, although she wasn't sure her dry throat would produce any sound at all.

''Scream all you wish,'' he said against her skin. ''No one will come, not when I made it clear we were to be left alone together after dinner. Now be still.''

His other hand moved upward, lifting the fall of honey-blond hair away from her neck, letting it slide through his fingers. Then his thumb began to stroke the soft skin of the nape of her neck, sending strange tremors through her body that she was unable to resist or control. His lips moved downward with warm deliberation to linger where the first swell of her breasts showed above the rounded neckline of her dress.

She said imploringly, ''No—Damon—please.'' But her words went unheeded. His caressing hand left her neck and slid down her back, taking, she realized with thumping heart, the zipper of her dress with it. His fingers stroked her spine, sending her body arching involuntarily against his, and he laughed deep in his throat.

''I liked what I saw at the hotel, *kóugla mou.* I want to see more.'' His voice roughened. ''I want to see all of you.''

She gave a little protesting moan, shaking her head, as his fingers dealt with the single clip fastening her bra and slid it, with her dress, off her shoulders.

For a long, long moment he sat staring at her in si-

lence, the pressure of his fingers on her wrists increasing
so intolerably that she sank her teeth into her bottom lip
to stop herself from crying out with the pain of it. Then
he raised his head and looked into her eyes. His own
were as dark as night, slumberous with desire, little
devils dancing in their depths. As their glances met and
held, Helen felt her breathing quicken, and was sham-
ingly aware of her bared breasts rising and falling swiftly under the force of the strange and incomprehensible
sensations that had her in their grip. Almost convulsively she closed her eyes, shutting out the sight, but not the
image of him. That seemed imprinted indelibly on the
back of her eyelids.

"Tell me, Eleni," his voice gritted. "How many men
have seen you as I see you now? How many?"

She wanted a retort that would shock him, but she
could think of nothing to say. And perhaps if she hadn't
been quite so clever with some of her earlier answers,
she would not now be suffering the most traumatic
humiliation of her life.

He said, "Answer me, damn you."

"None." A little shudder went through her. "No
one—ever."

"So—you are a virgin?"

"Yes." She whispered the sound, her mouth trembling, and felt that paralyzing grip on her wrists relax,
found herself released. Dazedly she opened her eyes. He
was no longer beside her or even near her. As she
watched him uncomprehendingly, he picked up his glass
from the table, tossed back its contents with a practiced
flick of the wrist, and set the empty glass down.

When his eyes met hers again, they were stranger's
eyes, cool and dispassionate.

"We shall be coming into Phoros in about ten
minutes," he said almost offhandedly. "When you have
tidied yourself, Dimitri will show you where you can

wash if you want, and comb your hair. I am going on deck."

She dragged her dress up to cover herself, her hands fumbling as she tried to deal with its fastenings.

"You can go to hell, and the sooner the better," she said raggedly, and saw that sardonic smile twist his mouth again.

"If you must have a focus for your displeasure, better me than your grandfather," he said.

"You—mean—that's what all—this was about?" She couldn't believe it.

"Not entirely," he said coolly. "I required the answers to a few questions, as well."

"Oh, I see." Her voice was quivering with irony and suppressed rage. "I understand. I do hope I've satisfied your curiosity."

"You've satisfied nothing," he said, and there was a note in his voice that sent the blood rushing to her face. "But it will do for a beginning."

"Not the beginning," she said. "The end, Mr. Leandros. The very end, I promise you. I shall never forgive you for this."

"For what? For depriving you of the satisfaction I have also denied myself?" he questioned mockingly. "Calm yourself, *kóugla mou*. Our time will come, and that is my promise to you."

He was at the door, his hand already reaching for the handle as she snatched up the empty glass and hurled it at him. Her aim was good in spite of her temper, but he was too fast for her, and the glass struck only the closing door, shattering into a hundred crystal fragments.

Helen sank back onto her seat. Though she hadn't hit him, the smashing of the glass had been the catharsis she needed, and she burst into a passion of weeping.

SHE WAS OUTWARDLY CALM and composed at least when she went up on deck to catch her first glimpse of Phoros. All traces of her storm of tears had been washed away in the elegant little compartment Dimitri had shown her to. No doubt he had also formed his own opinion of the smashed glass and her disheveled appearance, Helen thought angrily, but as she was never likely to see him again, it couldn't be allowed to matter much.

Damon Leandros was leaning on the rail, looking across the dark ripple of the water to the solid bulk of the land. She joined him silently, not looking at him, leaving several feet of careful space between them. She could see lights on the shore and guessed they were from the shops and *tavernas* bordering the small waterfront. It was warm and still, and she thought she could hear the sound of voices and laughter coming across the water to them as the cruiser crept forward between the strings of launches and caïques at their moorings.

She stared at the twinkling lights. There were others, too, farther away, and she wondered if one of them was the villa where presumably her grandfather was waiting. She bit her lip, and a little shiver went through her.

"Are you cold?"

She had thought his attention was fixed on the approaching shoreline and the slender dark cheroot he was smoking, yet he had been watching her. She felt herself stiffen as she said no, with ice in her voice.

"Then you are nervous?"

"Much as I appreciate your attempts at polite conversation, Mr. Leandros, I'm afraid that you're wasting your time." She spoke rapidly, not looking at him. "My one wish is to get off this boat, and hopefully never set eyes on you again."

"I cannot grant your wish." His voice was laconic. "I have to escort you to the villa."

"There is absolutely no need," she said. "If I were

you I'd put as many miles between my grandfather and yourself as you can." She heard him laugh softly, and clenched the rail in front of her so tightly that her knuckles turned white. "You don't believe that I'll tell him, do you?"

"Yes, I believe you. And, of course, you must tell him what you wish."

"So good to have your permission," she flashed.

He made no reply and after a while turned away, sending the butt of his cheroot spinning into the sea. She remained there alone, staring at the growing panorama of the lights and the small figures moving against them with eyes that saw nothing.

There was a car waiting on the quayside when they went ashore. Helen was surprised to see it. On the map Phoros looked too small to warrant motorized transportation. This time there was no uniformed chauffeur at the wheel, merely a stockily built young man in a short-sleeved shirt and faded jeans who gave Helen a long look of burning admiration before turning to shake hands, grinning, with Damos Leandros.

Damon said dryly, "Eleni, this is Kostas who works for your grandfather. He speaks little English, but if you talk slowly enough he should be able to understand you."

"Would he understand enough to throw you in the sea if I asked him?" she asked bitterly.

He sighed impatiently. "No, nor would he obey you if he did understand. Stop behaving like a peevish child, Eleni."

She gave him a furious look, and stood in seething silence while her cases were safely stowed in the car's capacious trunk. Then Kostas turned to her with a brilliant smile as he opened the rear passenger door for her. Damon Leandros got into the front of the car, leaving Helen in solitary splendor in the back. Kostas jumped into the driver's seat, let in the clutch with a jerk, and they started off.

The car negotiated its way along the quayside, then turned inland up a narrow village street. There seemed to be a number of people around, and most of the shops they passed were open for business even though it was so late.

She leaned her head back against the comfortable upholstery and closed her eyes, trying to ignore the incessant jolting as the car bumped its way over the rough surface. Once clear of the village, the road improved a little and Kostas picked up speed. Helen had been faintly amused when she first got in the car to see an array of religious medals, and even a small wooden icon fixed to the dashboard, but now as the car flung itself around bends with total disregard for any traffic that might be coming in the opposite direction, she began to wonder uneasily if the religious symbols so displayed were there for active protection.

They were still traveling inland, and climbing, as well, she noticed. She stared out at the moonlit landscape with a feeling of unreality. The scenery was barren with tumbled boulders lining the road, but here and there were clumps of trees that she supposed were olives. It looked bleak and alien, she thought apprehensively, yet her father seeing it with an artist's eyes had said it was beautiful. But then he had also been in love, she reminded herself, and a small sad smile touched her lips as she thought of her mother who had been born here, but had turned her back on it forever one sunlit day.

She closed her eyes again, and must have dozed a little, because the next thing she was aware of was the car slowing and turning off the road. She sat up with a start, peering out of the window, but there was still nothing to see. They were now on a narrow track that wound downward between groves of trees, and the mountains were behind them. They must have come across the entire island, she thought, because straight ahead she could see the moonlit glimmer of the sea.

Damon looked around at her. "You are nearly at the end of your journey, Eleni. We are now on your grandfather's land."

She made no reply but sat upright, gripping her hands together in her lap with painful intensity. All her doubts and fears returned in force to plague her as below them lights came into view. Damon Leandros had spoken only of reconciliation, but how did he know—how did anyone know what her grandfather really felt? Supposing he had invited her here to this remote place to exact some strange retribution of his own for being her mother's daughter? She told herself she was being a fool, but the thought hung around in her head, tormenting her.

Then the car was stopping, and there was no time to think anymore. Kostas got out and came to open her door. His smile was cheerful and reassuring even though he was a stranger to her.

The villa at first glance was a low rambling place with a tiled roof and white walls. Looking up Helen saw that a gallery ran around the upper story, and that a terrace surrounded the ground floor. Two shallow steps led up to the front door, which stood open, light spilling out in what she could only hope was welcome.

She swallowed and walked up the steps, aware that Damon Leandros was only one step behind her. As if on sentry duty, she thought almost hysterically.

Two women stood in the hall as she entered hesitantly, both dressed in black. But that was the only resemblance. The first woman, took a step forward, her held-out hand small and undeniably plump, her thick gray hair dragged back into a bun. Her eyes were filled with tears as she gazed at Helen, and with a little wail she snatched up the broad white apron she wore and covered her face.

"Her name is Josephina. She was your mother's nurse," Damon said in Helen's ear. "She is weeping for joy at the sight of you," he added somewhat caustically. "Say something kind to her."

Helen bit her lip, conscious all the time that the other woman, tall and smart in a haggard way, was exhibiting no sign of pleasure at her arrival. On the contrary, the dark eyes were coldly inimical as they studied Helen from across the hall.

Helen found her voice. "Dear Josephina," she said gently. "My mother spoke of you so often." And was glad she did not have to lie. Memories were stirring— memories of bedtime stories and her mother's voice telling her that she had heard such and such a tale from Josephina. She knew that her mother had loved her nurse and grieved because she had been forced to leave her behind.

Damon spoke again. "Kýria Atrakis," he said, and Helen realized with a start that the woman regarding her with such hostility was Thia Irini. "Will you take Eleni to your brother."

He spoke slowly in English, Helen realized for her benefit, but the woman replied in Greek, and even Helen's untutored ear realized the answer was a definite negative. She glanced at Damon and saw his face darken with anger.

He said, "If Kýrios Michalis is truly asleep, then we will obey the doctor and not disturb him. But I think that on tonight of all nights, *kýria*, he will be awake. And I think you know that, too. Come, Eleni."

His hand was under her elbow. She wanted to pull away, but was reluctant to do so in front of this strange woman who was her great-aunt, and who clearly did not want her here, who had not held out her hand or uttered one welcoming word as far as she could understand.

The floor they walked across was tiled in marble, and the stairs were marble, too, she noticed as they climbed them, with gracefully shaped pillars supporting a broad smooth rail. At the top of the stairs, galleries led off in both directions, and there was an archway directly ahead of them leading to a broad corridor with large double doors at the end. It was down this corridor that Damon led her. She was shaking inside, and some of her turmoil must have communicated itself to the man who walked beside her, no longer touching her.

He said, "You have nothing to fear, Eleni. He is your own flesh and blood. Never forget that."

He knocked quietly at one of the massive doors. It opened slightly and a woman in a nurse's uniform appeared, her face questioning as she peered at them, then lightening into a smile.

She took Helen's cold hand in hers and pressed it warmly.

"Welcome, *thespinis*. Kýrios Michalis has been impatient for your coming, and that is not good. Now perhaps he will rest."

Gently she drew Helen forward into the room.

CHAPTER FOUR

SHE STOPPED just inside the door, momentarily dazzled. The lighting in the corridor had been subdued, but this room was like a stage set, complete with principal actor.

He sat, propped up by pillows, in an enormous bed that stood on a slightly raised platform at the end of the room. It was a large room lighted by a huge central chandelier, but in addition two tall wrought-iron lamps flanked the bed. It was completely wild. Over the top, she told herself, yet at the same time not out of keeping with the man whose setting it was.

He was a big man, and although illness had slightly hunched the powerful shoulders, it had not otherwise diminished him. His hair was white and curled thickly still all over the massive head set on a broad neck. His nose was hooked and his chin jutted ominously. Beneath shaggy brows as white as his hair, his eyes were alert and bright as burning coals.

He stared at her, his eyes encompassing her greedily, almost unbelievingly. She saw his lips move. Guessed rather than heard the single word they framed. "Maria." And she saw that the brightness in his eyes was tears.

Something in her throat closed up and she swallowed convulsively, standing as if rooted to the spot. Then the nurse was there, bustling forward.

See, Kýrios Michalis, here is your granddaughter come from England to visit you. And if she will promise not to make you tired, I will leave you with her."

Michael Korialis turned his head slightly to look at her and said one short succinct phrase in Greek, which sent the nurse scurrying from the room with a scandalized squeak.

His gaze came back to rest on Helen, and she saw with relief that he had regained his self-command at least on the surface.

"The woman is a fool but her intentions are good," he said. He lifted a commanding hand. "Come here to me, Eleni." His voice was deep and rather harsh. It was a voice more used to order than to plead, she thought as she crossed the wide expanse of bedroom floor and mounted the single step to the platform.

He patted the counterpane. "Sit here. Let me look at you, *pedhí mou*."

She said steadily, "I can look at you, too, grandfather."

He took her hand in his. His hand was big and swarthy, the knuckles prominent. Her own looked pale and fragile against it. There were marks on her wrists. Marks that Damon Leandros had left on her flesh, but he was not looking at them. His eyes were searching her face eagerly, looking for further traces of her resemblance to her mother, she realized without resentment.

He said slowly, "Child of Maria, I cannot undo the past. It exists and I cannot change it even if I wished to, which I must tell you I do not. Your mother did me a great wrong. She also wronged the son of my friend."

"Because she fell in love with my father—whom I love, too," Helen said.

"Your father," he muttered. He took a strand of honey-blond hair and held it in his fingers for a moment.

"Yes, I have his coloring. Does—does it distress you?"

"No," he said heavily. "No, it is over, as I have said.

It is in the past. I must look to the future now, Eleni, if only because the doctors tell me I have so little of it left.''

"That's very hard to believe," she said honestly.

"Yet you must believe it. I am only thankful that you have come—that you are with me to share it—until the end." His voice deepened slightly, and he leaned back against the pillows as if the effort he had made so far had wearied him. Helen studied his face with concern. In spite of the strength and apparent power, the dominance she had noticed when she'd entered the room, there was at the same time an underlying frailty, she now realized. A frailty that for obvious reasons he preferred to conceal. She swallowed against the rising surge of unexpected emotion that threatened suddenly to overwhelm her. She wasn't sure what had prompted it, but Michael Korialis might interpret it as pity, which she knew it wasn't. She sat quietly on the edge of the bed, her fingers still clasped in his, watching some of the harshness and strain relax from the swarthy autocracy of his features.

When he spoke again his voice was barely above a whisper, and she had to bend her head close to his mouth to catch his words.

"Don't leave me, *pedhí mou*. Promise me that."

"Of course, I won't leave," she protested. "I've only just got here." She cast him an anxious look, wishing the nurse would return. He seemed quiet enough, his color was normal as far as she could judge, but she knew so little about grave illness. Supposing he was to suffer another attack now. Panic closed up her throat at the prospect, and a kind of grief, as well. This first contact had been brief, and there would be problems ahead, she knew, but she wanted the relationship to continue, to grow as far as it could, considering their differences in age and culture. It was too soon to talk about love, but there were the stirrings of sympathy within her, a desire to understand this fierce proud old man.

His breathing was deep and steady, and she thought he was falling asleep. Her hand was still in his and she was afraid that if she tried to withdraw it, he would waken, so she sat still, waiting for his grip to relax.

But it did not relax, and after a while the strain of sitting in one position without moving began to tell on her in cramped muscles. She was weary, too, with the long journey, and emotionally tired, as well, after everything she had been called on to endure.

She bit her lip. She hadn't mentioned Damon Leandros to her grandfather. It had simply not been right or appropriate to do so, and there would be time enough, although perhaps she would have to temper the bald truth a little out of consideration for Michael Korialis's health. But obtaining his dismissal was simply a pleasure deferred, she told herself defiantly.

Her eyelids were becoming impossibly heavy, and it was an effort to hold her head upright. She hesitated for a moment, then slipped her feet noiselessly out of her sandals and, moving cautiously, swung her legs up onto the bed, curling herself into a ball. The silky luxuriousness of the quilt was coolly comforting under her cheek as she settled as comfortably as possible. She wouldn't really go to sleep, she assured herself as waves of drowsiness assailed her. She would just doze a little until someone came. After all, she couldn't leave her grandfather alone.

It was to be her last coherent thought. Later she was dimly aware that she was being carried, and that there was an odd familiarity about the arms that held her, but perhaps that was all part of some strange disturbed dream. There was a woman's voice, almost cooing in its affection and concern, and warm, gentle hands ridding her of her dress and underclothes. Her attempt to speak, to ask where she was and what was happening was instantly hushed, and she capitulated without a struggle. There was a pillow beneath her head, and the touch of fine linen bleached with the sun and scented with wild thyme. She turned her face into its caress with a little muffled sound of pleasure and slept like the dead.

IT WAS BROAD DAYLIGHT when she finally awoke, and the sun was slanting fiercely across the bedroom floor between the slats of the shuttered windows.

Helen stretched slowly, pushing back the sheet that covered her, looking down at her lawn-nightgowned figure in some astonishment. She propped herself up on one elbow and looked around her, assimilating her surroundings.

It was a large room, simply furnished, which was in some way a reassurance. She had found the opulence at the hotel somewhat oppressive. The floor was tiled in an attractive mosaic pattern, and there were several rugs woven in shades of cream. The walls of the room were washed in a color somewhere between gold and pale apricot, and curtains and draperies in a vivid blue provided an attractive contrast. The bed on which she lay was a simple divan, rather lower than she had been used to in England, and the table beside it was large and square and highly polished. It held a tall ceramic lamp with a cream shade, and a covered glass jug with a matching beaker containing fresh fruit juice. She drank thirstily, wiping her mouth like a child when she had finished.

Then she climbed from the bed and went across to the shutters, pulling them back. Directly ahead of her sparkled the Aegean, a deep and radiant blue paling to turquoise where it merged imperceptibly with the sky on the horizon. She could see a strip of creamy beach bordering, as far as she could judge, the gardens of the villa itself. Everywhere she looked there was color—the vivid green of grass where sprinklers turned to counteract the prevailing aridity, the paler, silvery color of clumps of olive trees, the rainbow shades of flowers and shrubs, including the brilliant mauve of the unknown climbing plant that festooned the balcony outside her room.

She took a deep breath. The air was like crystal and fragrant with blossom and citrus.

She thought suddenly of her mother, and wondered whether Maria had ever, amid the grime, fumes and pollution of London, ached for one breath of this beauty and clarity and fragrance.

A knock at the door behind her startled her back to the present, and she turned hastily as the door opened and Josephina entered smilingly.

"So you are awake. That is good. The *kýrios* said you should be allowed to sleep for as long as you wished."

"That was thoughtful of him," Helen tried to smile in response.

"Thoughtful?" Josephina cast up her hands. "When you return as a blessing to us. Because of you Kýrios Michalis has spent his most peaceful night for many weeks, and the doctor is most pleased. Now he wishes to see you."

"I'll get dressed at once," Helen said.

"It is the doctor who wishes to see you, little one. You were ill yesterday, *ne*? He wishes to assure himself and Kýrios Michalis that you are recovered."

"But there's no need," Helen protested. "I'm perfectly all right. I just overdid the sun rather, that's all."

But for all her smiling amiability, Josephina was implacable. The *kýrios* had ordered that Thespinís Eleni should see the doctor, therefore if she would get back into bed, the doctor would be summoned. Helen found herself obeying with no very good grace.

The doctor was a stout middle-aged man with a thick mustache and deceptively mournful dark eyes. He was punctilious in welcoming her to Phoros, and took her pulse, temperature and blood pressure while keeping up a gentle flow of inconsequential chat about the contrasts between England, where he had studied for some time, and Phoros itself. He was courteous and thorough, and Helen found herself answering his questions with equal politeness. He tutted reprovingly over her escapade in Athens.

"You must take more care, *thespinís*, especially in the middle of the day. It is best to rest then in the shade. Were you not told this?"

"Yes," Helen admitted reluctantly. "But I wanted to do some sight-seeing and it was the only opportunity."

He smiled, the dark eyes still lugubrious. "Well, you have learned your lesson, *ne*? And now you will wish to bathe and lie in the sun. Well, you may do so, but by degrees if you please. Ten minutes, no more, the first time, *thespinís*. Your skin is pale and fair. To burn and blister it would be a crime as well as most painful for you."

"I'll remember," Helen promised, slightly amused.

He raised a knowing eyebrow. "You think I fuss perhaps. If I do, *thespinís*, it is not, forgive me, altogether for your own sake. Your grandfather must not be made anxious in any way. That is most important. I think your coming here will do nothing but good, if you can remember that. Humor him, *thespinís*. Later today he speaks of getting up from his bed. He wishes to eat with you upon the terrace."

"Is that wise?" Helen felt a stir of alarm.

The melancholy eyes held a sudden twinkle. "I think, *thespinís*, that to agree will cause less harm than to oppose him. You will not, of course, allow him to tire himself or become agitated." He saw her nod a little hesitantly, and began to close his bag with a satisfied manner. "That is good."

She said, "Thank you, doctor, for all the good advice. I'll try and stay out of trouble from now on. But I feel I've wasted your time, although it was kind of my grandfather to think of it."

On his way to the door he shot her a surprised look. But Kýrios Michalis knows nothing of it, *thespinís*. It was Kýrios Leandros who requested me to call on you."

She stared at the closing door, aware that her jaw had dropped. The nerve, she raged inwardly, gazing unseeingly into space, the unmitigated bloody gall of the man. She supposed it was intended as a conciliatory gesture of some sort. Well, he was mistaken if he thought she could be so easily won over after the way he had degraded and humiliated her.

But probably, it wasn't that at all, she thought contemptuously. He was just pretending concern, in the hope it would reach her grandfather's ears.

She sat bolt upright suddenly as an unwelcome memory returned to her. Josephina had put her to bed, she knew, as if she were a child, but who had carried her from her grandfather's room. She found herself hoping with all her heart that it had been Kostas, but deep within her was a nagging suspicion that she hoped in vain. The man who carried her had been no stranger, she thought, swamped by helpless anger.

She schooled her features as Josephina came bustling back.

"You wish to take your shower now? See, the bathroom is here, and there are towels and soap and lotions for your skin."

There most certainly were. Helen's eyes widened incredulously. The appointments of the bedroom might be simple, but the bathroom was lavish in the extreme, even to the extent of having a sunken tub as well as the tiled shower cubicle. Nor had she ever seen such an array of essences, perfumes and dusting powders, all bearing the names of famous French houses.

The shower was wonderful. Not too hot, just warm enough to be refreshing as well as cleansing, but Helen was a little taken aback when she pushed open the glass door to find Josephina waiting to envelop her in one of the huge fluffy bath towels. Flushing, she began an awkward protest that got nowhere because she was being toweled so vigorously she found speech impossible. Then she was enfolded sarongwise in another huge towel, and told that her coffee awaited her in the bedroom.

There was a plump dark-eyed maid there, making the bed with deft efficiency. Josephina poured out the coffee and handed Helen a cup. As she took it Helen was startled to see a glimmer of a tear on the older woman's cheek, and was immediately seized with compunction. Had she hurt Josephina by her obvious embarrassment at the personal services that the woman was clearly accustomed to offer?

She said gently, "Jospehina, you'll have to be patient with me. I'm just not used to being waited on in quite that way."

"Ah, no, *thespinís*. It is just... when your mother was a tiny baby I became her nursemaid. As she grew up it was my joy to serve her, so kind, so sweet, so beautiful. When she left I grieved for her. Now that you are here it is as if my little Maria has returned to me. I am a foolish old woman. Forgive me."

"There's nothing to forgive," Helen put down her cup and hugged the plump little figure, her own eyes suddenly moist. She managed a chuckle. "But I warn you I could get used to being waited on."

The maid who had been following the conversation with a puzzled frown, now broke in with a flood of giggling Greek, as her eyes moved with frank admiration over the creamy skin of Helen's bare shoulders, and the damp tendrils of honey hair clustering around her neck.

"*Pó, pó, pó.*" Josephina wagged an admonitory finger at her, but she smiled indulgently just the same. "Yannina is right, *thespinís.* She tells me that my presence here will not be needed for very long. That you will have a husband to share your waking moments."

Helen laughed aloud. "I think your job's safe, Josephina," she said, aware that she had blushed slightly. "I have no plans to get married in the foreseeable future." She saw a shadow of bewilderment on Josephina's face and hastened to make her meaning clearer. "No husband, Josephina, not for many, many years."

The girl Yannina spoke again, clearly asking a question that Josephina silenced with an urgently lifted hand. Helen was aware of a subtle change in the atmosphere that she could not explain.

"Is something wrong?" She looked from one to the other with brows raised inquiringly.

"*Óchi. Me sinhórite.*" Josephina rather peremptorily signaled Yannina to be gone, and she scuttled away. "Pardon me, Thespinis Eleni. It is just that. . . for one so young and so lovely there must be a husband waiting."

"No," Helen shook her head. "I promise you there isn't." She thought of Christopher whom she had been dating desultorily before her grandfather's summons. She had enjoyed their pleasant undemanding relationship. He hadn't been too pleased when she had announced her intention of leaving for Greece, but she had no doubt that he would have found suitable consolation already, and certainly marriage had been the furthest thing from either of their minds.

When Josephina had departed, Helen took her coffee and her chair onto the balcony, sitting it, mindful of the doctor's instructions, in the shade of the trelliswork that separated her part of the gallery from that of the adjoining room. There were bees busy among the blossoms, and their humming produced a sense of pleasurable languor in her.

As she had laughingly told Josephina, she could soon get used to this kind of life. But she mustn't allow herself to do that. She was here for a month, and then it was back to an English autumn and her work at the gallery. Later she would write to her father and tell him of her safe arrival and first impressions of Phoros. She bit her lip. She would not, however, mention Damon Leandros. There was no point. There was nothing Hugo could do about him, and her father was probably anxious enough already about her.

Her main problem now was how to reveal the truth about Damon Leandros to her grandfather without agitating him too much. On the face of it, it seemed an almost impossible task. She remembered the firm lines of Michael Korialis's mouth, the still aggressive jut of his chin, and sighed a little. Supposing he did not believe her?

Perhaps there was someone else whose support she could enlist in advance. The doctor, maybe? She considered that and shook her head. He also took orders from the arrogant Mr. Leandros.

And there was absolutely no point in asking her great-aunt for any help, if her reception last night had been anything to go by. Helen frowned in bewilderment as she remembered the blank hostility in the older woman's face. Yet as far as she could recall, her mother had always spoken of her father's sister with affection, or perhaps that might just have been the gloss applied by distance. She wished she had been older when her mother had spoken of her family, then she might have known the right questions to ask, and might have come here with a shrewd idea about the levels on which the various relationships were conducted.

She drank the rest of her coffee and went back into the bedroom to get dressed. The crumpled navy dress and the undies she had worn had already been removed for laundering, she realized. Her cases had been unpacked, and their contents stowed in the fitted closets. She reached for a pair of white cotton jeans and a sleeveless top, then paused. The doctor had mentioned that her grandfather proposed to have a meal with her, and it occurred to her that tight-fitting jeans that hugged her slender hips and made the most of her long legs might not be the most tactful choice. A rebellious voice in her head argued that she should start as she meant to go on and wear what she wanted without regard for outworn conventions about dress. But tempting as the thought was, she dismissed it. The conviction that her grandfather would not approve of women wearing trousers, no matter how attractive, prevailed, and the last thing she wanted was to upset him, especially about such a trivial matter.

Instead she picked out a cream flared skirt, teaming that with the simple dark green top, its neckline deeply scooped at the front and back. Her damp hair had dried out on the balcony and she brushed it so that it hung smoothly to her shoulders, curving slightly toward her face. She applied moisturizer and added a touch of green shadow to her eyelids, deciding that the heat made other cosmetics inappropriate.

When she was ready she opened her bedroom door and peeped into the corridor outside rather cautiously. There was a bell in her room, and she had no doubt that if she rang it someone would appear with the speed of light to guide her downstairs with due ceremony, but she decided she would prefer to find her own way. She walked along to the end of the passage and found she was standing on the gallery overlooking the main reception hall. She began to descend the stairs slowly, taking in her surroundings with more attention than she'd been able to give them the previous night.

There was a marvelous feeling of space and height, she thought, and very little embellishment or ornamentation. Whoever designed the house had decided to let the beauty of the stone speak for itself.

She hesitated when she reached the bottom of the stairs. Several doors opened off the hall, which was deserted, and Helen glanced around her. One of the doors would lead to a dining room, she supposed. She tried the nearest door and found it opened onto a large sitting room, furnished with a number of low sofas in cream hide. There were fur rugs on the tiled floor and one end of the room was dominated by a large open fireplace—a reminder that the weather on Phoros could attain a certain bleakness in winter, although she would not be here to see it, Helen told herself. She walked across the room and stood staring out through the sliding-glass doors that led onto the terrace she had noticed the previous night. As well as the festoons of climbing plants, there were stone urns planted with blossoms all along the terrace.

Helen pulled the heavy door open and stepped out into the sunlight. Bees droned among the blossoms, and farther away in the garden she could hear the eternal rasping of cicadas. The stone of the terrace's balustrade was warm under her hands as she leaned on it. A smile curved her lips. It was like a foretaste of paradise, she thought.

"Kaliméra, Eleni."

He had come around the corner of the house so silently that she had no advance warning of his approach, and was standing on the flagged path underneath looking up at her.

Helen felt herself recoil as violently as if one of the laboring bees had floundered out of the blossom and stung her.

"Oh—it's you." She hunted not too successfully for a semblance of composure. He looked tough, virile and amazingly arrogant in brief bathing trunks that clung to his lean hips. His bare feet were thrust into heelless leather sandals and a white toweling jacket was hung carelessly around his shoulders, emphasizing his deep tan and the thick mat of hair that covered his chest, tapering into a vee across his flat abdomen.

She allowed her lips to curl slightly. "Dressed for a hard day's work, I see."

"I'm going for a swim before taking lunch with your grandfather. Do you wish to join me?"

"No, I don't, thank you." She paused. "And perhaps I should warn you that I'm also having lunch with grandfather. Your company will not be required. In fact I'm surprised that you're still here."

He smiled. "Perhaps I don't frighten as easily as you think, Eleni. And I have every intention of remaining here until your grandfather asks me to leave."

"Bravado, Mr. Leandros." Helen forced herself to speak coolly. "You're hoping that concern for my grandfather's health will keep me quiet, and that you can . . . brazen things out somehow."

"You may tell your grandfather whatever you wish, Eleni. Your little threats have no fear for me."

"You're very sure of yourself, aren't you?" she said angrily. "Well, remember this, Mr. Leandros. No one is indispensable."

She turned and went back into the room behind her, pushing the door shut with unnecessary force, furious with herself for having been drawn into another confrontation with him.

She crossed the room and went into the hall, pausing

irresolutely as she tried to decide what to do next. Somewhere near at hand a woman was talking, her voice high-pitched and voluble. She was speaking in Greek, so Helen could not understand what she was saying, but her tone was sharp and almost hysterical. Every so often there was a long pause, and Helen realized she was listening to half of a telephone conversation. She also realized that if anyone came into the hall, they would find her standing there apparently eavesdropping. She flushed a little, and moved toward the stairs intending to return to her room to wait until her grandfather sent for her.

She heard a distant tinkle of a receiver being vehemently replaced, then a door to the left of the one she had just emerged from was wrenched open, and Thia Irini came into the hall. She was dressed in black from head to foot as she had been last night, and she carried a handkerchief that she was jerking through her fingers.

She stopped as soon as she saw Helen, and a heavy frown descended on her brow.

"Ti thélete?" she demanded, her attitude no more friendly or welcoming than it had been when Helen first arrived.

Helen spread her hands. "I'm afraid I don't understand," she said quietly.

She was surprised to see an expression of relief pass quickly across the older woman's face, and wondered if Thia Irini's half of the recent conversation had included any uncomplimentary remarks about herself.

At last Thia Irini said slowly, "Something...you want?"

"Not really." Helen shook her head. "I just wondered where everyone was, that's all."

Thia Irini shrugged in an uncomprehending manner, but Helen had the strangest feeling that she understood her much better than she wished to admit.

She wanted to cry out, "What's the matter. I'm my mother's daughter and she never spoke of you with anything but affection. Why don't you want me here?"

But she remained silent. Damon Leandros was enough of an enemy for her to cope with at the moment. Perhaps Thia Irini was simply concerned for her brother's health and considered her arrival an unnecessary disturbance. Maybe when she realized that Helen was only there as an act of reconciliation, she would soften and become more amenable.

I certainly hope so, Helen thought ruefully as she gave her great-aunt a rather strained smile before turning away.

As she reached the gallery she met the nurse.

"Ah, *thespinís.*" The woman smiled and nodded at her. "You slept well, I think, and so did Kýrios Michalis. We must thank you for that. Today he is so well, so happy." She laughed. "He wishes to show you everything, I think. The villa, the grounds. It will be difficult to make him rest."

"Oh, dear," Helen pulled a slight face. "The last thing I want is for him to overexert himself. I will be careful."

"But yes, *thespinís.* No one would doubt that. It warmed the heart to see you together last night. Kýrios Leandros was much moved, that I could see."

Helen was about to declare tartly that she was wholly indifferent to Damon Leandros and his reactions, but she checked herself just in time. The last thing she wanted was to cause talk or speculation of any kind while she was at the villa. Besides, there had been that certain note in the nurse's voice when she referred to Damon Leandros that suggested that his attractions had not been lost on her.

I hope I'm not breaking up a beautiful friendship, she thought wryly as she followed the other woman along to her grandfather's room. It was not quite so dramatic in daylight with the lamps extinguished and the bed neatly made. The French windows were open and Michael Korialis was sitting in a chair beside them, his hands clasped lightly on a silver-mounted cane. He looked around as Helen entered, and held out a hand to her.

"Hérete, pedhí mou." There was a small stool standing near the bed and he indicated that she should bring it nearer. She placed it at his side and sank down on it, aware rather uncomfortably that the nurse was observing every move with an indulgent smile.

"You slept well," he said, more as a statement than a polite inquiry. "You look well, you have more color today. Our Greek sun agrees with you, it would seem."

"Everything here agrees with me," she said gently. *Except one,* she thought inwardly, *and this isn't quite the moment to bring him into the conversation.*

"Josephina looked after you well?" he asked. "She was hardly more than a child herself when she came here to be nursemaid to your mother. She worshipped the baby. Maria took Josephina's heart, too, when she ran away. In you, she sees her beloved child restored. That is good."

Helen smiled a little. "As long as I don't break her heart again when I have to go home," she returned.

"This is your home." The black eyes under the shaggy brows flashed with sudden fire.

"I hope it is," she said. "But I do have another one in London, and I have to return there when this holiday is over. I thought that was understood when I agreed to come here."

She met her grandfather's glare with apparent equanimity.

"Already you talk of leaving," he grumbled in an undertone. "Phoros does not appeal to you?"

"It's beautiful." Helen felt they were on dangerous

ground and tried to shift the emphasis of the conversation. "Is there only the one small port? How many people actually live here?"

He shrugged. "Not many. There are a few villas used by busy men as their retreat as mine is. I built this villa for your grandmother. I wanted our children to grow up away from the city. I thought we would end our days here together. If I had realized how long I would be alone here, I think I would have torn it down to its foundations." His hand came down on her shoulder. "Do not leave me alone here, Eleni."

She hesitated before replying. It was clear that her grandfather was trying to obtain some kind of commitment from her and this was something she did not feel able to give. She had promised to spend a month here, but that was all. Somehow she had to make him realize that she had a life, responsibilities she could not ignore even if she wanted to, back in England. Her father needed her, and not simply because she filled a vital role at the gallery. She'd heard the phrase 'tug of love' many times, she thought with a sense of despair, and hadn't realized it could apply to adults as well as children.

She tried to smile. "Grandfather, you're not being fair. Let's just take each day as it comes, and make the most of every minute. Now where are we going to have lunch? Out on your balcony?"

"I think I would like to eat downstairs." Michael Korialis gave the discreetly busy nurse an openly defiant look. "There is an arbor with a view at the end of the terrace. It can be pleasant there. And Damon will be joining us," he added with evident satisfaction.

Helen, out of the corner of her eye, saw the nurse pick up a tray with medicines and head for the door. She smothered a sigh of relief.

"Can't we have lunch alone—or just with Thia Irini?" she added quickly.

He gave a grunt. "My sister will not eat with us. She dislikes meals taken in the open air." He gave Helen a narrow look. "It is my wish that you become better acquainted with Damon."

Helen bit her lip, repressing an urge to inform him that she had nearly been more intimately acquainted with Mr. Leandros than even her grandfather could wish.

She said, "Did you know that he asked me to go swimming with him earlier?"

"You did not accept his invitation?" Her grandfather sounded faintly amused.

"No." Helen paused, then settled for ambiguity. "I wasn't sure if it was. . . safe to do so."

Michael Korialis chuckled. "Our gardens lead to a beach that belongs to this villa. There are no currents or dangerous rocks, *pedhí mou*."

No, Helen thought, *but deeper waters possibly than I have any intention of getting into*. She smiled up at her grandfather. "That's very reassuring," she said.

"Then the next time Damon invites you to swim with him, you will go?"

Taken aback, Helen said, "Why there may not be a next time. He may not ask me again."

There was a rumble of laughter. "I think he will, my little one. Oh, I think so."

He sounded almost approving, Helen thought with sudden apprehension, and that was something she had to put a stop to right now. She'd wanted to choose her own time—the right time to make her accusation against Damon Leandros. Something told her this was too soon, but the initiative had been taken away from her.

She said clearly, "I hope he doesn't ask me, grandfather. I find him totally detestable. I don't want to worry you or upset you but I've got to tell you that you can't trust him."

"What are you saying?" The hand on her shoulder tightened suddenly.

Helen swallowed. All the gleeful anticipation she had imagined she would feel had vanished. Instead she was the stranger, the intruder, bringing bad news about a man her grandfather knew well and relied on deeply.

She said, "I don't know exactly what his duties are around here, but I don't think making passes—trying to make love to your female relatives—is among them. His behavior to me in London and on the journey here has been despicable."

There was a long silence, and when she ventured to look up at him, he was frowning, his shaggy brows drawn heavily together.

"Are you telling me that Damon has become your lover? This, I do not believe."

"Oh, no," she said hastily. "I don't think even he would dare to go that far—but he—he kissed me—and—and humiliated me in other ways." She was miserably aware that the sense of outrage that had driven her so far was withering under the realization that her complaints were making her sound like an insufferable little prig. And she hoped that Michael Korialis would not make her specify the "other ways."

"You find it humiliating for a man to demonstrate that he finds you desirable?" Her grandfather's tone was dry suddenly. "I had not thought that young English women led such sheltered lives. Your compatriots who come to Greece on holiday give a different impression."

"You—you sound as if you're defending him." She shook her head in bewilderment. "I thought—I took it for granted that you'd be angry that one of your employees, however highly you thought of him, should paw me around. I assumed you would fire him."

"Fire him?" He stared down at her as if she had gone mad. "What is this you are saying?"

"It's slang," she said miserably. "It means—dismiss him from your employment—dispense with his services. Call it what you like. At any rate it means get rid of him."

The grip relaxed on her shoulder. He was shaking all over, she could feel it, and apprehension seized her. Had she made him ill again by her disclosures, brought on another attack?

She made herself look up at him again, and her eyes widened in incredulity. Michael Korialis wasn't shaking with temper, but with laughter, leaning back in his chair, eyes closed, and giving way uninhibitedly to his enjoyment.

"Ah, *pedhi mou*," he said at last, recovering himself sufficiently to pinch her cheek jovially. "Someone has been having a little joke with you, I think. I cannot— fire Damon Leandros."

"Why not?" she persisted. "It isn't. . . he hasn't got some kind of hold over you, has he? Is that why he thought he could behave as he did with me?"

"No, no, my little one." He was laughing again. "Calm your fears, Eleni. Who has been filling your head with this nonsense? And who has told you that Damon is in my employment?"

"Well, he did—at least I think so." She was stammering a little as she tried to remember what had exactly been said. Had Damon Leandros actually claimed to be working for her grandfather or had she taken it for granted? She began to feel slightly sick. "You mean— he doesn't work for you?"

"He does not. He has no need to work for me or for any other man," her grandfather retorted wryly. "When his father, who was my friend, died, he was already a millionaire. And when his older brother, to whom I was also close, was laid to rest, he inherited the remainder of the corporation. He could buy this island, if he wished, or my entire chain of hotels.''

''I see.'' Helen felt numb. ''So the jet—the motor cruiser—they all belonged to him.'' She forced a smile. ''You're quite right. Someone was having a joke with me. In fact Mr. Leandros was amusing himself at my expense. But then, I suppose anyone as rich as he must be can do exactly as he pleases.''

''It would certainly be a brave man who chose to oppose the wish of his heart. But he is my friend, Eleni, and our families have always been close.'' She could hear anxiety in her grandfather's tone, but was there a note of warning, as well. Was he trying to tell her that Damon Leandros would make a bad enemy?

''He will never be my friend, grandfather,'' she said slowly. ''But for your sake I will try to be civil to him at least.''

The nurse came back at that moment, suggesting diplomatically to Helen that she might wish to wait for her grandfather downstairs. Helen guessed that Michael Korialis might have difficulty in rising from his chair unaided, and would not wish her to see this evidence of a physical weakness that she imagined he despised. He approved of strength, and of the strong, she thought as she went downstairs, and this was probably why he liked Damon Leandros. Her instinct told her that if Damon had been a weakling or a fool, her grandfather would have had no time for him, no matter how rich he might be.

She started violently as she realized on reaching the foot of the stairs that the object of her thoughts was standing in the doorway opposite, watching her. He had changed, she noticed. He was now wearing cream close-fitting denim pants and a navy shirt unbuttoned at the throat, and his hair glistened with dampness.

He was smiling, too, she recognized savagely. He knew as well as if he had been an unseen eavesdropper in that sunlit bedroom upstairs what had transpired between Michael Korialis and herself, and was amused by it. From the first he'd been amused, she thought, her temper rising. It had been a game to him—taking her misapprehensions and playing on them deliberately—feeding her just enough rope to ensure that she would at least make an attempt to hang herself.

Damn him, she thought wildly, her fingers involuntarily bunching into fists at her sides. And because he was a valued friend of her grandfather she would have to put on a show of civility, have to smile and pretend to share the joke, starting with this blighted lunch party.

His smile widened as if he could sense her inner turmoil, pick up her vibrations, read her thoughts.

"The sea was like silk, Eleni. You should have come with me. But there will be other times. I look forward to showing Phoros to you."

It was her turn to smile—a polite stretching of the lips that he would rightly interpret as totally meaningless.

"That's very kind of you, Mr. Leandros, but thanks to my grandfather I've imposed far too much on your time and patience already." The words of a polite child, she thought with inward satisfaction, and saw his eyes narrow.

"It will be my pleasure."

"But not mine." Something in his tone, its faint arrogance perhaps, needled her. "The fact that you are a rich and important man, Mr. Leandros, hasn't changed a thing as far as I'm concerned. Your company is still completely unacceptable to me."

She saw his dark brows draw together swiftly. Anger, she thought triumphantly, and a touch of incredulity, too. Physically dynamic, sexually attractive, wealthy—up to now he must have thought he was irresistible.

"Is that so?" he said at last. "And yet there have been moments—particularly on board the *Phaedra*—when I gained a very different impression."

His eyes traveled deliberately down her body, reviving memories she would rather have left buried in her subconscious. The color flared in her cheeks, and she heard him laugh softly. "Was I wrong, Eleni?"

"Oh, no." By some miracle she managed to sound quite cool, even controlled. "I'm sure you'd make a marvelous lover—very practiced, very expert," she added with a curl of her lip. "But I'm not in the market for a lover—and I'm not for sale, either, in case that's what you were thinking."

He smiled again, but it had altered. It was no longer amused, and it certainly did not reach his eyes.

"As you pointed out, I am a rich man, but I did not become so by offering to buy commodities I could obtain for nothing," he said, and Helen heard herself gasp at the insult. His voice continued relentlessly, "If I want you, Eleni, I shall take you, so stop trying to deceive yourself."

"You are vile." Her voice shook. "Get out of here—get away from me."

"As you wish." He shrugged as if it was a matter of supreme indifference to him. "A lunch party would seem inappropriate under the circumstances. Perhaps you will make my excuses to your grandfather."

"It will be a pleasure," she said between her teeth, and turned abruptly to go back up the stairs—anywhere, she told herself, away from the sight and the sound of him. And noticed as she did so another movement. On the other side of the hall, a door was closing smoothly and quietly, as if pushed by a draft or an unseen hand.

Helen paused, gripped by sudden uneasiness. Had there been an unknown witness of the confrontation between Damon and herself? She hoped not. Even if the eavesdropper spoke no English, the tone of their voices would have left no doubt that they were quarreling, and a report might go to her grandfather. And only a few minutes before she had promised she would be civil to Damon Leandros.

He, of course, had gone. The hall was empty behind her, and sunlight spilled across the tiled floor through the open front door. She hesitated for a moment, then walked across the hall to the door she had seen moving. A stray draft on this golden windless day? She didn't think so. Someone had been there listening. She pushed open the door. The room was empty—the dining room, she noticed in passing—and the French windows to the terrace stood open, so anyone wishing to avoid discovery could have beaten a retreat that way.

Helen sighed. She did not regret one word that she had said to Damon, but she had no wish for it to come to her grandfather's ears. She could only hope the eavesdropper would keep whatever information had been gleaned to himself.

She walked across to the terrace, but it was deserted. It was evident, however, that this was where she was to have lunch. A small trellis-shaded pergola had been constructed at this end of the terrace, and a table had been set there with a snowy linen cloth and silver cutlery. Set for three, she noticed, her lips twisting.

She sat down on one of the slatted wooden benches in the pergola while she rehearsed what she would say.

"Damon couldn't stay, grandfather. He asked me to give his apologies. He's been called away on urgent business."

Perhaps a tinge more regret on her part to add conviction, but otherwise it was a reasonable explanation for his absence, and far better than admitting the bald truth—that she had driven him away because.... She paused. Because she hated him? Was it really as simple as that?

Yes, she whispered to herself. *It really is that simple. I'll never forgive him for what he did to me—for the way I was humiliated.*

She heard the murmur of voices inside the villa. Her grandfather must be on his way. She schooled her face to receive him, taking a firm grip on her composure, and tried to ignore the small mocking voice in her head that told her that although she could not forgive him, she was going to find it even harder to forget him.

CHAPTER FIVE

"THE LAST TEN DAYS have simply flown past," Helen wrote to her father.

> I haven't seen a great deal of the island yet, because naturally I've been spending as much time as possible with grandfather, and although he seems much better, he's still restricted to the house and grounds on doctor's orders. I swim every afternoon at a private beach, and I'm developing quite a tan, but I'm taking it easy as it would be very easy to burn.

She put down her pen as she considered what to say next. At the moment she seemed to be treading a precarious path between the unvarnished truth, and the kind of lighthearted relaxed chat her father would be expecting and hoping for.

In fact the time hadn't flown. It had dragged rather. Oh, not when she was with her grandfather. Her time with him was always interesting and enjoyable. She shared all his meals. They talked, they played backgammon. They were slowly and carefully constructing a relationship. It couldn't be hurried. Apart from the age gap, their lives had been lived in different environments—almost different planets, Helen thought sometimes. Their experiences, their expectations, of each other, were often poles apart, so they were proceeding with care.

But when she was alone, she was very much alone,

and the hours hung heavy on her hands. Apart from her daily visits to the beach, she was also pretty much restricted to the house and grounds herself. She sighed. She had expected she would be able to visit the village. Kostas, after all, drove over there regularly, she knew. But somehow it was never convenient for her to accompany him. In fact it was almost as if the village had been declared out-of-bounds for her, although she told herself she was being overimaginative about this.

She supposed, too, that it made a certain amount of sense for her to remain close to the villa. If her grandfather were to be taken ill again and need her, she didn't want to be several miles away. But even the doctor said he was making remarkable progress, and professed delight with his improvement. So perhaps she wasn't being unreasonable when she wished she could be let off the hook, just for a little while.

If she'd had something to do—someone else to talk to even—while her grandfather was resting, things would have been different, she thought. But there was nothing and no one, except for Josephina whose conversational topics were limited. Helen enjoyed hearing her talk about her mother as a baby and a small child, but even the fascination of that palled after a while.

And Thia Irini, it had to be admitted, avoided her. Helen had made overtures, had tried halting Greek hastily learned from Josephina, but all to no avail. Her great-aunt seemed to regard her with implacable hostility, and her rather timid offer to help with the household duties had met with an open rebuff. Her face flamed as she remembered it. She hadn't intended to interfere or imply that the running of the villa left anything to be desired, but that was the interpretation that Thia Irini had chosen to place on her words, according to Josephina's frankly embarrassed translation of her great-aunt's hissed reply. Remembering her glaring eyes, and the tone of her voice, Helen thought ruefully that her reply might well have been played down by Josephina, and was glad that she didn't understand more than a few simple Greek phrases.

But all this would change when Madame Stavros arrived in the next day or two, and in spite of her protests that she did not need a tutor/companion, Helen found she was looking forward to her arrival more than she could have believed possible. She had been expected more than a week ago, but had been delayed by a summer virus.

Of Damon Leandros, there had been no sign since he had walked out of the villa that day. Michael Korialis had grumbled about his continued absence, but had accepted her original explanation without question.

Helen told herself that he would keep away until she was safely back in England, but she was oddly on edge each day just the same, and the image of him intruded on her thoughts far more than she even wished to admit. She supposed he would have returned to Athens and found herself wondering if the dark-haired beauty she had seen in his car that day was with him. Her gibe that she could not be bought had been foolish and unnecessary, she thought. He would never need to buy a woman, even though she had resented the arrogance of the assertion at the time. She wished she could press a switch and blot him out of mind and memory, or at least stop this endless recital inside herself of everything they had said to each other. At least when Madame Stavros came she would have something else to occupy her mind.

She picked up her pen and ended her letter to her father, thrusting it into an envelope and sealing the flap. Presently she would leave it with the rest of the outgoing mail on the table in the hall, but what happened to it after that was anyone's guess. She supposed Kostas

Your **FREE gift** *includes*

Sweet Revenge by **Anne Mather**
Devil in a Silver Room by **Violet Winspear**
Gates of Steel by **Anne Hampson**
No Quarter Asked by **Janet Dailey**

FREE Gift Certificate

and subscription reservation

Mail this card today!

Harlequin Reader Service:

Please send me my 4 Harlequin Presents books free. Also, reserve a subscription to the 6 new Harlequin Presents novels published each month. Each month I will receive 6 new Presents novels at the low price of $1.50 each [*Total - $9.00 per month*]. There are no shipping and handling nor any other hidden charges. I am free to cancel at any time, but even if I do, these first 4 books are still mine to keep absolutely FREE without any obligation.

CP120

NAME	(PLEASE PRINT)

ADDRESS

CITY	STATE / PROV.	ZIP / POSTAL CODE

Offer not valid to current Harlequin Presents subscribers.

Offer expires December 31, 1981

PRINTED IN CANADA

Take these 4 best-selling Harlequin romance stories FREE

exciting details inside

took the letters into Kyritha as part of his other duties, and that all the mail left for the mainland on the evening ferry, but she couldn't be sure, and her grandfather was clearly bored by discussion of such mundane details as the operation of the island's postal system.

She got up and walked over to her bedroom window, thrusting her hands into the large patch pockets on the front of her skirt. She was wearing a cotton dress today, dark red and sleeveless with a low neckline and full swirling skirt. She was thankful that her instinct to concentrate on feminine clothes in her luggage had been fully justified. Her grandfather's reaction to her appearance in jeans had been exactly as she had suspected, so she was careful to avoid them in his presence, although she usually wore them for her beach excursions.

She wandered out onto the balcony, and stood looking around her. She was bored, there was no denying it. Her grandfather always rested in the morning and lunch on the terrace was a long way off. She had to find something to occupy her. There were no English books or magazines at the villa, but surely there would be some in Kyritha. On at least one day there was a market, she knew, because she had heard her grandfather mention it. There would be stalls selling dress material perhaps, and she could buy some and make herself a wraparound skirt, and maybe a blouse, as well. Josephina had an elderly sewing machine—and at least it would be something to do.

She glanced irresolutely at her watch. She had better take her letter downstairs or Kostas would leave without it. Perhaps she could persuade him to buy her some material, if she described what she wanted—drew a sketch of the kind of pattern. Helen took a breath.

"This is utter nonsense," she announced to the room at large. "I'm not a prisoner here. I can go into the village myself." She grabbed up her handbag and went out of the room.

Kostas was in the hall, arguing cheerfully with Josephina over the contents of a list she had just given him. He flashed Helen a wide smile as she descended the stairs, holding out his hand for the letter she was carrying.

She withheld it, returning his smile. "Today, I would like to go with you, Kostas. I want to do some shopping in Kyritha."

She had spoken slowly, and he should have understood her perfectly well, but instead he turned to Josephina frowning, obviously asking a question. Josephina looked concerned, too.

"There is little to see in Kyritha, *pedhí mou*. Kostas will bring you anything you need."

"But I want to go." Helen stood her ground. This was the kind of argument that had been put forward on other occasions. "I want to buy some dress material. He can't choose that for me. Besides, I'd like to see Kyritha. So far I've caught one brief glimpse of it, and that was at night. There are shops aren't there? And *tavernas*? I'd just like a change of scene for an hour or two. We'll be back in time for lunch won't we, Kostas?" She smiled at him again, but his broad face was unhappy, and he avoided her gaze, looking appealingly at Josephina who shrugged in resignation and said something to him in Greek.

"Oh, for heaven's sake," Helen broke in impatiently. "I'm not asking to be taken to the moon, just to the village. What's the matter with the place. A plague epidemic hasn't broken out there has it?"

Josephina said something in a low voice about it not being the wish of Kýrios Michalis.

"That's utterly ridiculous," Helen said. "I'm sure you must have—misunderstood him Josephina. But if that's what you think—well, it can be our little secret, if you like. Kostas will get me back here well in time for lunch, and Kýrios Michalis need never know anything about it.''

Driving away from the villa, beside a plainly sullen Kostas, Helen reviewed the situation in some bewilderment. So she had not been imagining things, after all. It seemed that her grandfather had indeed declared the village out-of-bounds for her. But why? There seemed no sense in it. Her grandfather could not expect a girl of her age, brought up in total freedom as she had been, to meekly submit to dividing her time between the villa and its beach, as if the outside world did not exist.

The thought struck her that perhaps Michael Korialis was afraid that she might follow in her mother's footsteps and elope with a comparative stranger, and a small derisory smile touched her lips. That was nonsense, if so, and he must be aware of it.

She would have to talk to him frankly, she decided, and make it plain she could not be expected to pass her days like a nun in a convent. She would also put his mind at rest, if necessary, about the possibility of her finding romance in Kyritha. Who did he visualize her with, she wondered suppressing a giggle. Another artist or a young Greek fisherman all bulging biceps and tarstained vest? The whole idea was ludicrous, and a little sad, as well.

She settled back in her seat to enjoy the scenery. For such a small island it was quite spectacular. The road they were traveling on had been carved out of the side of a mountain, she noticed, and on the other side the hillside fell away to the valley floor several hundred feet below. Down there the scrub and boulders gave way to clumps of trees and cultivated fields. There was a house, too, half-hidden among the olive and citrus groves, a sprawling villa like the one they had just left, but even more palatial from the glimpse she could catch of it and the turquoise gleam of a swimming pool close beside it.

There was little other traffic on the road, and that was just as well because Kostas's method of driving was heavy on the accelerator and light on the brake. Helen found herself holding her breath as they rounded some of the bends. Prudently she transferred her attention to the mountain instead, staring up at its shimmering cloud-crowned summit. Its upper slopes were bare rock, gleaming in the sun in shades of gray, pale green and amethyst. Against the blue arc of the sky a solitary bird wheeled and hovered at the sight of prey moving in the scrub far beneath. Helen closed her eyes as the bird swooped. She didn't want to know whether its dive of death had resulted in success or failure. This was raw country, uncivilized and barbaric in spite of the man-made road, and it made her feel uneasy and alien.

She was almost glad when she saw the red roofs of Kyritha shining below them and the sapphire sea beyond. She sent Kostas an encouraging smile but his expression remained glum.

"Look," she said reasonably. "If you're worried about what Kýrios Michalis will say, I'll explain to him. I'll tell him that I made you bring me, you had no choice. Will that do?"

He shrugged and muttered something, but he was plainly far from mollified. Clearly her grandfather's word was law with his employees, and it had been her duty to accept it without question.

Some chance, she thought. *Grandfather is a darling in many ways, but he's still an autocrat deep down. If he ruled mother like this, it's no wonder that she ran away.*

As Kostas parked on the waterfront, Helen saw delightedly that the little market was in full swing. She climbed out of the car and, waiting only for a fat man wearing a beret to wobble past on his bicycle, ran across the road to the first stall.

It wasn't the most wonderful market. There were several stalls selling cheap jewelry and rack on rack of worry beads. One trestle table was totally covered by pots and pans and the simpler kind of kitchen gadget, while others were festooned with cushions, curtains and lace tablecloths in rather garish colors and patterns. Business was far from brisk, but no one seemed particularly worried, and one stall holder at least was snoring gently in his folding chair. Helen supposed that things would improve when the morning ferry from the mainland arrived with its quota of tourists. She turned abruptly and almost cannoned into Kostas who was standing right behind her.

"It's all right," she assured him patiently. "Go and do your shopping. I'll be fine. I'm just going to have a look around, and then have a glass of lemonade in one of the *tavernas*. We can hardly miss each other."

She was convinced he knew exactly what she was saying, but he continued to follow her, his expression mulish.

Oh, hell, Helen thought in exasperation. *The last thing I want is a keeper dogging my heels and glowering all the time.*

She tried again. "Kostas, please. I'm just going to stroll around. I'd rather be on my own. Alone."

Kostas shook his head, his mouth set firmly. "Kýrios Michalis would not permit," he said.

"I've never heard such nonsense," Helen said roundly. "Kostas, I live in London. I've never needed a bodyguard there. Why should I want one here? Surely my grandfather hasn't got that many enemies?" she added, trying to smile.

Kostas's shrug said it all—that her arguments counted for nothing, it was not for him to reason why, but he had his instructions and would carry them out. And he had been clearly instructed not to let her out of his sight. Helen felt like screaming. She gave Kostas one fulminating look, then turned and stalked away, her chin in the air.

"Excuse me." A voice. An English voice. "Is this man bothering you?"

Startled, Helen swung around. He was tall, she saw at once. He towered head and shoulders above the bristling Kostas at her elbow. Tall, and undeniably good-looking, and smiling down at her with immense charm.

He said, "If this man is giving you trouble, I can get rid of him."

Helen returned his smile. "Actually it isn't as bad as it looks. Kostas works for my grandfather. He's only doing his duty as he sees it. It's just unfortunate that I see it rather differently."

"Your grandfather?" His brows rose. "My God, then you must be the Korialis girl."

Helen's smile froze a little. "No, I'm the Brandon girl."

He said wryly, "I'm sorry. That must have sounded terrible. I've been listening to too much local gossip."

Helen stared at him. "You mean—you're not on holiday."

"Good Lord, no. I live here, and have done for several years. I run a *taverna* on the harborside." His smile widened. "What's the matter. Don't you believe me?"

Helen said rather shakily. "Oh, yes, I believe you. What I can't believe is that no one at the villa told me that there was one of my own countrymen living in Kyritha. Apart from my grandfather himself, there's been no one I can talk to in words of more than one syllable since I arrived. But then it must be equally limiting for you."

"Yes, although I do speak Greek. But now that we've stumbled across each other, may I buy you a drink?"

"I'd like that," Helen agreed. She turned to her companion. "Kostas, I'm going to have a drink with Kýrios..." she paused, sending the newcomer an interrogative look.

"Lassiter. Craig Lassiter."

"With Kýrios Lassiter. I'll meet you at the car later."

For a moment she thought he was going to protest, and nerved herself, wondering how on earth she was to deal with it. Then red-faced, and sending Craig Lassiter a look of uncompromising hostility, Kostas turned and trudged away, muttering as he went.

Helen said, "Honestly," as she watched him go. She turned to Craig Lassiter, moving her shoulders rather helplessly. "I'm sorry about that. It seems he's had orders to watch me like a hawk."

"It's a sensible precaution. Your grandfather's a very rich man. If someone snatched you, they could expect a considerable ransom."

"You're not serious."

"Not entirely, no. But I suppose it's always something that has to be considered. At least that's the view that Mr. Korialis would take."

In spite of the heat Helen felt as if someone had laid a cold hand on her shoulder. She exaggerated her slight shiver, trying to laugh.

"I—I didn't realize I was quite such a marketable commodity. I shall have to bear that in mind."

Craig Lassiter gave her a concerned look. He put a hand lightly under her elbow, guiding her over the few rough blocks that formed the pavement. "I hope I haven't worried you."

"Of course not." Her denial was instant, but she hastened to change the subject just the same. "What made you choose Phoros to settle in?"

He grinned. "The natives seemed friendly. And the climate, of course. Apart from the occasional thunderstorm, it's generally as glorious as it is today all summer long. I can recommend it," he added with a sidelong look. "It's even mild here all winter."

"I won't be around in the winter." Helen gave him a quick smile. "I'm only here for a few weeks, or hadn't local gossip established that?"

"Oh, I think you've been marked down as a future resident. It's generally reckoned that you'll be persuaded to stay, one way or another."

"I'm afraid not." Helen shook her head decisively. "It's a beautiful place, of course, but I have my father and my career waiting in London."

Craig Lassiter said lightly, "No one else?"

She flushed a little. "Not really. My local dossier would seem to be incomplete."

"Don't you believe it. Your future husband has already been chosen for you." He stopped, his hand tightening on her arm. "Well, here we are. 'A poor thing, but mine own.'"

"It's charming," Helen protested as she looked around. It wasn't the largest establishment on the waterfront, but it was sparkling clean, with a mint-fresh green-and-white-striped awning over the doorway. Inside the *taverna* Helen could see a long gleaming bar with a glass top, and a few tables covered with green-plastic tablecloths. At the back of the room a beaded curtain over an archway led to the kitchen at the rear, she guessed. There were more tables set just outside on the pavement, and double the number across the road on the harborside itself.

"We do quite well," Craig agreed. "It gets quite hectic when the ferry comes in, but because there's so little accommodation for tourists on the island, we have our quiet periods, too. It suits me very well. Choose your table, and I'll bring you your drink. How do you like ouzo?"

"Not a great deal." Helen wrinkled her nose candidly. "Could I have a glass of wine?"

"Retsina?" There was a trace of challenge in his voice.

She laughed. "Yes, why not? I've had it before." She paused suddenly as the exact circumstances of that first time came back to her.

"What's the matter? You looked for a moment as if you'd seen a ghost."

"Just an unpleasant memory," she said rather defensively. "I'll wait for you across the road."

Nearly all the *tavernas*, she noticed, had alfresco extensions on the seawall, their gay overhead awnings supported by a complex of scaffolding poles.

Helen felt rather conspicuous as she sat down. Sitting in the sunshine in the midmorning, enjoying a drink, seemed to be a masculine prerogative, and she was the target of some unsmiling looks from the occupants of tables at neighboring establishments. She was glad when Craig, carrying a tray crossed over to join her.

"When in Greece..." he commented as he set down two glasses of iced water in addition to the retsina. "You don't have to drink it, if you don't want to. It's Loutraki water, however, and I can recommend it."

"I know it already." Helen smiled. "My grandfather drinks a great deal of it."

"Of course," he said on a faintly satiric note. "Nothing but the best for the rich men of Phoros." He saw her surprised look and gave a half-apologetic shrug. "I'm sorry if I sound a little jaundiced, but you're part of that setup, aren't you? You couldn't be expected to know what life can be like on the island for we lesser mortals."

Helen's brow wrinkled. "You mean they give you a hard time? My grandfather included?"

"Your grandfather in particular," he corrected her, smiling rather ruefully. "It hasn't been easy being English on Phoros, for reasons I'm sure I don't have to go into. I'm hoping for an improvement in relations from now on."

"I can't really say very much to defend him," Helen said in a low voice. "Except that he *is* an old man, and all his life he's been allowed to believe that every decision, every judgment has been the correct one." She made an effort to smile. "It doesn't induce a particularly reasonable attitude."

"But a fairly common one among Greek males, as you must have already discovered for yourself. Or have you been so bowled over by his charm that you haven't noticed?"

"I'm sorry. You've totally lost me," Helen said after a pause. "Are we still discussing grandfather?"

"God, no." He gave an explosive laugh. "I meant your prospective bridegroom."

"I really don't know what you're talking about." Helen put down her glass and stared at him frowning. "I have no bridegroom, prospective or otherwise. I'm not engaged, I'm not even going steady. What is all this?"

He said lightly, "More of that local gossip, I'm afraid. It seems you're expected to wipe out your mother's blot on the family escutcheon by marrying a man of your grandfather's choice in her place. Not the original choice himself, as I understand he was killed in an accident some years ago, but his younger brother, thus providing a neatly happy ending to what in Greek eyes has always been a messy and rather shocking story."

Helen sat very still. Her mind was hard at work,

remembering remarks that had been made, making connections between facts that she had only vaguely assimilated. She could hear her grandfather's voice, "Our families have always been close." Recalled his mentioning an older brother who had died, and his anxiety that she and the surviving member of the family should be friends. Or more than friends.

She said with a calmness she was far from feeling, "It's Damon Leandros, isn't it? The man I'm—intended to marry. How stupid of me not to have guessed."

"Look." Craig Lassiter reached across the table and touched her fingers with his. "It may only be a rumor. How much of it is true, and how much wishful thinking on the part of the locals. . . ."

"Oh, I think it's probably true." She managed a wintry little smile. "It all makes too much sense."

It explained only too well her grandfather's mild reaction to the news that Damon had been making love to her, she thought. Presumably a few liberties were permissable with one's bride to be. She remembered Damon's voice demanding to know whether she was still a virgin, and hot angry color stung her cheeks. No doubt if she had answered in the negative—and how she wished she had done just that—plans for the marriage would have been quietly dropped. And she remembered the maid Yannina's obvious bewilderment when she had laughed at the very idea of having a husband. Everyone, it seemed, knowing everything, except herself.

"Are you all right?" Craig queried sharply. "You look almost ill. God, I'm sorry. I should have kept my mouth shut."

"Oh, no." She met his gaze steadily. "I'm grateful to you, actually. Forewarned is forearmed, after all."

"I see." A note of amusement entered his voice. "Am I to infer that you don't welcome the prospect of becoming Mrs. Leandros? I reckon that probably makes you unique. From all accounts, he can choose any woman he wants, and frequently does.''

''I'm well aware of that.'' Helen had a brief image of the dark beauty she'd seen in his car in Athens. ''It doesn't add to his attraction as far as I'm concerned. But you're quite right. I have no intention of marrying him, or anyone else for that matter.''

''Good for you,'' Craig said cheerfully. ''I wish you luck in the battles ahead. That's if there are any.''

''Oh, I'm sure there will be,'' she said ironically. ''Don't they say when Greek meets Greek then comes the tug of war? And I am partly Greek through my mother.''

And there was another saying, she thought. Something about fearing the Greeks when they came bearing gifts. Her original instinct to reject all Damon Leandros's overtures had been the right one. Instead she had allowed her curiosity to lower her defenses, and she had no one to blame except herself if she now found herself in an intolerable position.

''*Thespinís.*'' She looked up with a start to find Kostas standing over her. ''It is time we returned to the villa. Kýrios Michalis will be anxious. Please, *thespinís.* Come now,'' he added, giving Craig Lassiter an openly inimical stare.

Helen thought rapidly. She supposed she could refuse to return, and evade the inevitable search party, so that she could leave on the next ferry, but that wasn't a satisfactory solution to her problem. It would mean leaving her clothes and most of her personal belongings behind, not to mention her passport. Besides, she had very little money with her, and certainly nothing like the cost of her air fare back to Britain, and she had to be practical. She would have to write to Hugo and ask him to book her a seat on a return flight from Athens and send her the ticket. But that would take time, and in the meantime she would go quietly on with her holiday as if she was totally unaware of the plans being made for her future.

She rose, picking up her bag, and Craig got up, as well.

"Do you have to go?" he asked in an undertone. "I was really beginning to enjoy this morning."

"I don't want to worry my grandfather by being unnecessarily late," she said quietly. "And there'll be other mornings. I've enjoyed this, too."

Kostas was muttering under his breath all the way back to the car.

"You should not have gone with that man, *thespinís,*" he said when they were on their way back to the villa. "It is not right. Kýrios Michalis will be angry with us."

"Then why bother to tell him?" she countered sweetly. "It's all right, Kostas. In my country women are allowed to have a drink with a man."

"But this is not your country, *thespinís,*" he said sullenly. "Besides..." he hesitated.

"Besides, Kýrios Leandros will also be angry?" she completed the sentence for him. But he isn't here, Kostas, so that doesn't really matter, either. And I don't care what Kýrios Leandros says, or does, or thinks, anyway."

And I hope that gets back to him, she thought vindictively, registering the look of shocked disbelief her companion turned on her, and a small satisfied smile curved her lips.

She had thought that after their quarrel, Damon Leandros had decided to go away and stay away, but in the light of what Craig had told her, she now wondered if he was just biding his time. He'd probably kept in touch with her grandfather all along, she thought, biting her lip savagely. Well, that didn't matter, either. It was

immaterial how many little victories he could congratu-
late himself on winning. The final one would be hers
when she returned to England, alone.

For a second the word "alone" and all its connota-
tions startled an odd pang from her, but she told herself
she was just being foolish. After all, she wasn't really
alone. Waiting for her in London was her father and the
life they had made together, just as if she had never been
away. Yet was anything ever as simple as that? Was she
really thinking that she could go home and pretend that
the last few weeks had never happened? She wasn't sure
she was even the same person, and she knew whom to
blame for that, she thought wearily. From the moment
Damon Leandros had walked into her life, she had felt
confused and apprehensive, and his subsequent behavior had only served to deepen the conflict in her
emotions. She told herself that she hated him, yet barely
a day passed when she hadn't thought of him at least
once. She was disturbed and bewildered by the way in
which images of him seemed to be taking control of her
mind, waking and sleeping. She didn't want to think of
him, yet he was always there hovering at the edge of her
consciousness, disturbing and bewildering her in his
absence almost as much as he had done when very much
present.

One night she had even dreamed about him—a dream
that had humiliated her to recall in the bright searching
light of day, leaving her feverish with longings she
didn't want to admit, even to herself. Her mouth went
dry as she remembered how real it had seemed, so real
that when she woke her body had moved restlessly
across the bed, unable to believe she was alone.

Alone. That word again, she thought, her mouth
twisting as she stared unseeingly out of the car window.
Why was she suddenly obsessed with loneliness?

She sighed under her breath, closing her eyes and

leaning back against the seat. They would soon be back at the villa, and she had to assume at least the appearance of tranquillity for her own sake as well as her grandfather's.

Somehow or other she had to find a diplomatic means of getting across to him that his plans for her were as doomed to failure as those he had made for her mother. It wouldn't be easy, she thought somberly, but the situation had been of his making, not hers. And Damon Leandros's continuing absence would help. Perhaps, after all, she was worrying about nothing. Maybe he had already decided that he had as little taste for this proposed marriage as she had. With luck she might never even have to see him again.

Beside her, she heard Kostas give a little exclamation in his own language. Rather wearily she opened her eyes to see what had attracted his attention, and her first thought was that she had fallen asleep and was dreaming again. Because, impossible as it seemed, there was a helicopter standing on the smooth green lawn in front of the villa. She leaned forward, staring in disbelief.

"See, *thespinís*." Kostas sounded almost triumphant. "Kýrios Leandros has come. Is good, *ne*?"

Helen didn't reply. She was incapable of speech, and aware at the same time that her pulses were behaving most erratically. Because he was there. She could see him standing by the front door, watching the car approach, a pair of dark glasses concealing the expression in his eyes. He was casually dressed, with dark blue denim pants emphasizing the leanness of his hips and the strong length of his legs, and a matching shirt unbuttoned almost to his waist.

As Kostas brought the car to a smooth halt, he moved, descending the steps with easy grace. Helen began to fumble with the handle on the passenger door, but Damon was there before her. The door swung open,

and his hand was on her arm helping her out of the car.
She had to restrain a gasp as his fingers touched her bare
flesh. It was all too reminiscent, both of her dream and
the potent reality that had preceded it.

Abruptly she pulled away from him

"I can manage, thank you." Her voice was slightly
higher pitched than she had intended.

"As you wish, Eleni." His voice was smooth, and she
could read nothing from his tone. "Your grandfather is
waiting for you. He has been a little anxious."

"I can't think why. I'm quite capable of looking after
myself." But not, she thought wildly, when her heart
was hammering, and her legs were threatening to give
way under her as they carried her up the steps to the
front door.

Instinctively, but hating herself at the same time, she
looked around to see if he was following.

He wasn't. He was standing beside the car and Kostas
was talking to him in a low rapid voice, using many
gestures. Damon stood with his head bent, nodding
every so often as if to encourage Kostas's confidences.
Helen did not doubt that they concerned her. *He's telling him I met Craig Lassiter,* she thought.

And even as the realization crystalized in her mind,
Damon lifted his head and looked up at her, and she
was suddenly appallingly aware of an icy furious anger
that seemed to reach out like a blow from a mailed fist.

For a moment she stood there, weathering the storm,
her tongue flicking out to moisten her dry lips. Then
with a feeling of almost overwhelming relief, she heard
her grandfather's voice in the hall behind her, and she
turned and ran to him as if for refuge. She remembered
too late as his arms closed around her and his voice
began to scold her fondly for making them all wait for
lunch, that all she was doing was running to another
part of the trap that had been set for her.

CHAPTER SIX

HELEN LAY ON HER BACK staring up into the olive tree above her. It was her favorite spot on the beach beneath the villa, affording some measure of protection from the fierce afternoon heat. Here the sun only dappled through the branches, warming without burning, highlighting the long supple shape of the silvery leaves and the clusters of rounded fruit that nestled among them.

She thought, *mother—I love your country—and I've got to get away from it for exactly the same reason you did.*

She felt sudden tears prick behind her eyelids, and rolled almost defensively onto her stomach, pillowing her head on her folded arms. She fought weakness with anger, going over in her mind the events of the seemingly interminable lunch party she had just endured.

Damon had still been angry when he had joined them at the table in the pergola. She had known it, although she had to admit that he gave little obvious sign of it. He talked and smiled and joked with her grandfather, but all the time Helen was aware of tension simmering between him and herself. It unnerved her, and she only picked at the grilled sardines in a tangy lemon sauce that were served as the first course, causing Michael Korialis to comment chidingly on her lack of appetite.

Helen could only guess at the reason for his annoyance. She supposed it was because she had insisted on going to the village and had met Craig Lassiter there—but where was the harm in that? Unless he realized that Craig had told her about the proposed marriage plans, and that she would be now more than ever on her guard against him. There could be no other reason. Even if she had given signs that she was willing to docilely fall in with their schemes, Damon could not expect her to shun the company of all other men for the rest of her life, so such an attitude under the present circumstances was totally unreasonable.

He said very little to her, but as she forced herself to eat she was conscious of his eyes watching her intently, and her uneasiness grew. The tension lifted a little with the unexpected arrival of Thia Irini. It was the first time she had made an appearance at the lunchtime parties on the terrace since Helen's arrival, and Helen was frankly surprised to see that her usually vinegary expression had been replaced by as near an approximation of a beaming smile as the older women could manage.

Damon rose, kissed her hand politely, and seated her next to him with an air of great respect, after which it could be said that Thia Irini monopolized the conversation to Michael Korialis's obvious annoyance. She chattered to Damon showing more animation than Helen had thought she was capable of, and as the conversation was conducted solely in Greek, Helen felt absolved from the responsiblity of trying to take part in it and was able to become absorbed in her own disturbing thoughts.

From remarks her grandfather had made before the meal, it seemed that Damon had been invited to stay at the villa as his guest, and that the helicopter that had brought him would be leaving soon without him. She indulged herself for a while with fantastic plans to stow away in the craft, but she soon admitted that any such plan was unfeasible. For one thing, the helicopter might not even be returning to Athens, and for another, she had no idea if there was any form of cover in the thing that would conceal her until they had taken off. But even if there was she would be discovered sooner or later, she decided pessimistically, and the thought of being flown back to Phoros and dumped ignominiously back at Damon Leandros's feet was unbearable.

Somehow she had to find a way of getting through her remaining few weeks at the villa without upsetting her grandfather, at the same time avoiding Damon as much as possible. He was a proud and arrogant man, and surely if she continued to show him as plainly as possible that she wanted nothing to do with him, then any ridiculous notions he or her grandfather might harbor about marrying her to him would wither and die. She recalled what Craig Lassiter had said about him. When there were women in the world ready and eager to become anything he wanted them to be, then it was hardly likely he would continue to pursue a girl who made it clear that she found his company repulsive.

Besides, she told herself, she might just be reading a great deal too much into some harmless local gossip. It was only a small island and the doings of the wealthier inhabitants must be one of the chief sources of entertainment.

She hoped fervently that this was in fact the case. The story Craig had outlined had repelled her by its cold-bloodedness apart from anything else. If she'd understood him correctly, the implication was that the man her mother had been intended to marry had been Damon's older brother. She racked her memory trying to recall what Maria had said about this unknown prospective bridegroom, but all she could remember was that the betrothal had been presented to her mother more or less as a fait accompli. She bit her lip. Had the same thing been planned for her? Surely they must have known that her reaction would be exactly the same as Maria's—repugnance and flight.

Every so often Michael Korialis tried robustly to interrupt the conversation between Damon and his sister, speaking in English, and trying to draw Helen into it, too. But Thia Irini, Helen saw with some amusement, was not easily gainsaid. She continued to engage Damon's attention with a kind of determined intimacy, her slightly clawlike hands with their splendid rings touching his sleeve as if she was afraid his concentration might wander. Helen had to give him an unwilling ten out of ten for courtesy. He was charming to the older woman and deferential, and gave no sign of the impatience and irritation that was consuming Michael.

Although she could have sworn her name had never been mentioned, Helen was at the same time uneasily aware that the conversation seemed to concern her. Occasionally Damon's eyes flickered in her direction, and her grandfather's expression was openly anxious at times.

Helen wanted to say, "Look, it doesn't matter if she's uttering dire insults because I don't understand a word of it," but instead she took another forkful of veal stew, smiling innocently at her grandfather.

It was during the dessert, a kind of sponge cake flavored with almonds, that Thia Irini addressed herself to Helen for the first time.

"It is a pity you do not speak our language," she said in her slow fractured English. "You would learn many things that you should know."

Such as the fact that you don't like me, Helen wondered silently. *I don't need to speak Greek to understand that.*

Before she could formulate a reply, Michael Korialis spoke. "All that will change tomorrow when Madame Stavros joins us," he said repressively, and Helen saw Thia Irini's eyes flash with displeasure. "Eleni will soon learn to love and speak her mother's tongue."

Helen shook her head. "I wouldn't count on that, grandfather. I—I never was much good at languages, I'm afraid. And in such a short time. . . ." She shrugged expressively, her eyes fixed on her plate.

Damon said smoothly, leaning forward a little, "But where there is the will to learn, wonders can be achieved even in a small space of time. Wouldn't you agree, Eleni?"

"I really don't want to waste any of the time I have left here on lessons that will be wasted when I get home," Helen said levelly. "I'd rather spend it with grandfather. That was why I came here, or had you forgotten, Mr. Leandros?"

"I haven't forgotten—anything." His eyes were veiled, his expression enigmatic, but the warning in his cool tone was unmistakable, and she tensed.

Michael Korialis was smiling. "Your lessons would not be wasted, *pedhí mou*." His face was guileless. "This will not be the only holiday you will spend with me I hope. And another language is always an asset. There are many things that Madame Stavros can teach you."

Such as how to be a meek submissive Greek wife, Helen thought, schooling herself to surface tranquillity although she was inwardly seething. *Well, the good lady will find I'm remarkably stupid, I'm afraid.*

Lessons in Greek were to be the first step, she supposed, to be followed by expert tutoring in grooming and the finer points of etiquette. Anything, in fact, that the wife of a wealthy and powerful man would be required to know in order to fulfill her role completely, and keep his household running smoothly.

And if she hadn't caught that virus, Helen thought, *I'd probably have been lapping her lessons up by now. If I'd gone into Kyritha, then she would have been with me, and I would never have met Craig and found out what they were up to.*

She pushed her plate away and leaned back against the wooden slats that formed the back of the seat. As she did so she realized that Thia Irini was staring at her with a look of real malignance in her eyes. But why, Helen wondered helplessly. What on earth had she done to provoke such a reaction? In spite of the fact that her great-aunt knew, or admitted to knowing so little English, Helen had made every effort to be pleasant whenever they encountered each other, but from the first evening she had sensed this implacable hostility, and she was at a loss to understand it.

Damon was rising, excusing himself from the table with the brief explanation that he had to give the helicopter pilot some instructions before he took off.

"I shall rest," Michael Korialis announced. "What do you plan to do, *pedhí mou*?"

"I shall go on the beach as usual," Helen said reluctantly, guessing that her grandfather intended Damon to join her there when his business with the pilot was completed.

"You will not swim so soon after a meal," he said sharply.

"No, of course not." She appeased him with a smile. "But I want to make the most of the sun while I'm here. When I go home we'll be moving into autumn in England."

Her eyes lifted, full of innocence, to his face, and she caught the merest flick of a smile on his lips, a secretiveness in his eyes, and she had to look away to conceal the anger and disappointment in her own expression.

She had turned away and gone up to her room, angrily pulling off her clothes and strewing them on the floor as she hunted through the drawers for a bikini. She chose a black one she had not worn before, covering it with a hip-length black muslin shirt with full sleeves for her walk down to the beach. On one of her earlier sun-bathing expeditions, she had set off through the garden just in a bikini, and had come face to face with a young man who was delivering something to the villa. The way he had leered at her had made her feel hot all over, and now she took the precaution of adding a toweling jacket or a shirt before venturing out of doors. She slid her slender feet into a pair of heelless mules and collected her dark glasses, some lotion for her skin and a paper-back novel.

She had half expected to find Damon waiting for her in the hall downstairs, but the house seemed deserted, although she could hear Thia Irini's voice scolding someone—probably a hapless maid—somewhere in the distance.

She moved languidly through the sun-drenched garden. The paths were dusty again, although each morning they were hosed down to keep the worst of the dust at bay. The hum of the cicadas seemed almost drowsy in the intense heat. As she moved away from the house along the narrow paths flanked by parched-looking flower beds, she was conscious of an almost irresistible urge to look over her shoulder. Someone was watching her walk down to the beach. She knew it. She straightened her shoulders and lifted her chin. She had to appear tranquil and carefree at all costs, and innocent of what was going on to the point of dumbness, if that was necessary.

She shivered slightly in spite of the intensity of the sun, the memory of Damon's unspoken but nonetheless terrible anger surfacing in her mind. What could have triggered off such a rage, she simply could not comprehend.

Nevertheless the shadow of the memory seemed to hang over as she tried to relax on the beach. She opened her book, but the words danced meaninglessly in front of her unseeing eyes.

She thought on a gust of anger, *oh, damn and blast the man. I'm getting obsessive about him. I can handle the situation. There's no way I can be compelled into marriage against my will in this day and age.*

As she lay there in the shade of the olives, half dozing, she found she was repeating the last words over and over again in her head as if they were a charm.

She was so very nearly asleep that she did not hear his approach. The first sign she had was the splash of the cool liquid on her heated skin, and then, as she came awake, the shock of his touch on her exposed back, moving gently, massaging, as he rubbed the sunlotion into her flesh.

Helen sat bolt upright, her head spinning dazedly as she stared at him.

"Did I startle you?" he smiled, but without any particular warmth as he observed her instinctive lunge away from him across the straw beach mat and out of his reach. "The sun has moved, and your skin was becoming reddened."

"That is rather the purpose of the exercise." She stretched out her hand for the bottle of lotion, but he ignored her gesture.

"But it is dangerously easy to blister in this heat. You should protect your skin."

She wanted to say childishly that she would rather become one large blister than have him touch her again, but she remained silent, very conscious of the briefness of her bikini, and his eyes upon her.

After a while she said, "I suppose my grandfather told you where to find me."

"I would have come to the beach, anyway. I like to swim in the late afternoon."

"Then I'll leave you to it," she began, reaching for her shirt, but he detained her, his hand on her wrist.

"Won't you swim with me, Eleni *mou*?" Again his

smile did not reach his eyes, only wryly twisted the corners of his mouth.

"It's too soon after lunch," she said quickly. "I—I think I'll go for a walk instead."

"As you wish." He got to his feet in one lithe movement, and bent down to her, reaching for her hand to pull her upright, and she realized too late that he intended to come with her. "You wanted this?" He picked up her shirt and held it for her to slip her arms into the sleeves.

It was no real kind of protection, she realized ruefully, as she thrust her feet back into her mules. It was altogther too thin and flimsy, and it covered her only to the tops of her thighs, its sole fastening a button and loop at her midriff. It shielded her from the onslaught of the sun, but that was all. As a garment it was more provocation than anything else.

And the tormenting remembrance that he had seen her in even less only served to increase her self-consciousness.

His hands had seemed to linger on her shoulders as he had helped her put on the shirt, but he did not attempt to touch her, to take her hand or her arm as they walked along, and she was thankful for this without really knowing why. She had thought she would almost welcome a confrontation between them—to tell him she knew his plans and wanted no part of them, but now she was suddenly not so sure. She sensed a tension, a restlessness about Damon, and found herself wishing obscurely that she had stayed in the house where at least there were people within call.

He said abruptly, "If you continue to walk so fast, you will turn your ankles on the stones."

"Your concern for me is quite overwhelming," she flashed. "I mustn't get sunburned, and now I mustn't sprain my ankle. Anyone would think you had some kind of vested interest in my well-being."

Well, it was said, she thought, and it was too late to regret that sudden reckless impulse.

"My interest is to make sure that your visit here passes enjoyably. It would worry your grandfather if you were to become ill in any way."

Helen was completely taken aback by the laconic reply. She'd expected—what? Some kind of admission, a declaration? She wasn't sure. Her face burned. Perhaps Craig's story had only been gossip after all. If so she had come within inches of making an utter fool of herself.

They were walking away from the beach, she noticed, but the path they were taking was not one that led back to the house. It was rough and covered with loose stones, and it sloped upward among the crowding olive trees.

"Where are we going?"

"You haven't been this way before?"

"Well, no," she confessed. "I'd intended to do some exploring, but the beach has always been too beguiling."

"And also the village, it would seem." This time his glance was totally unsmiling.

"I've been to the village, yes." Helen lifted her eyebrows. "Is something wrong with that?"

"It is not a particularly lively place."

"But there **are** shops there. I wanted to buy some dress material."

"And you were successful in this?"

"As a matter of fact, no." Helen bit her lip. "There wasn't a great deal of time. Kostas seemed to be in a great hurry."

"Perhaps it was simply that he did not approve of the company you were keeping."

"He made no secret of it. I suppose it would never occur to any of you that talking to one of my own compatriots might make a refreshing change."

"You are wrong," he said. "Kyritha is a small village. If you went there it was inevitable that you and Lassiter would meet."

Her lips parted in silent outrage for a moment, then she said huskily, "So I was right. There was a deliberate policy to keep me away from the place. What's the matter? Isn't a *taverna* keeper good enough for me to talk to? Would it be better if he owned a longer string of hotels than grandfather's? Would it make him acceptable?"

He said wearily, "You talk like a fool, Eleni. Your grandfather has good reason for not wishing you to become too friendly with someone like Lassiter."

"Because he's English, I suppose." Helen gave a brittle laugh. "My God. I didn't realize quite how deep that particular prejudice went. Is he afraid that I'm going to take a leaf out of my mother's book?"

"I think he has a higher opinion of your intelligence than that," he said dryly.

"Then perhaps he had better be careful." Helen stopped in her tracks and swung to face him, her eyes furious. "I won't submit to the kind of pressure that he tried to inflict on my mother, either. I belong to myself. You might tell him that."

"I shall do nothing so hurtful," he said cuttingly.

"No," she said wretchedly, aware that she had allowed her temper to betray her. "But he must understand that things are different in England, I have to be allowed to choose my own friends."

"Even if the choice is an unwise one?"

"You don't like Craig?"

"You are more than perceptive, Eleni. No, I do not like him."

"Well, I do," she said defiantly. "I'm afraid your prejudices carry little weight with me. I like Craig, and I intend to see more of him while I'm here."

"Then it is as well that your time will be fully occupied from tomorrow. Perhaps you will be more receptive to Madame Stavros's guidance than to mine." He did not bother to disguise the grimness in his voice.

"I thought I'd already made my views clear on that, as well," she said. "Her coming here is simply a waste of her time and mine."

"You would prefer to waste your time with Lassiter."

Helen wasn't sure she wanted to go quite that far, but she said yes anyway, and was pleased to see his dark brows snap together in a heavy frown.

Emboldened, she said, "I won't be driven to do anything against my will."

"I would not count on that if I were you." He moved on, and Helen stood for a moment looking after him, strongly tempted to turn and go back the way they had come, if only to reinforce the point. But at the same time she was curious to know where they were going, so eventually she followed slowly.

The path became steeper, and Helen found herself having to scramble over the rocks that littered it. She noticed irritably that Damon did not look back to inquire if she needed a hand, not that she wanted any of his help, she assured herself silently, wincing as she scraped her knee against a jutting piece of sharp rock. She paused, flexing her leg a little and regaining her breath at the same time. A few yards ahead the path seemed to taper out as it reached a kind of ridge, and there Damon was waiting, leaning back against a tall boulder, a thin blue wisp of smoke rising from the cheroot he had just lighted.

Helen was suddenly aware of a strange silence. The rasping of the cicadas had hushed as if the whisper of the breeze that stirred the branches of the sheltering olive trees had murmured some charm commanding quietness. The brilliance of the sunlight seemed mellowed as it spilled through the silvery leaves, and on a flat rock a few inches from Helen's hand a lizard appeared in a flash of green and gold and lay, its only movement in its tiny panting sides, like a small armored sentinel. Somewhere she thought she heard the cooing of doves.

In spite of the languid heat of the afternoon, Helen felt herself shiver a little. She was an alien surrounded by forces she did not understand. Brownish red dust rose in little eddies as she climbed the last few yards where Damon still stood, his back half-turned to her. A pebble, disturbed by her foot rolled away down the slope with a crack like a pistol shot, and Damon looked around at her.

Their eyes met—locked, and her shiver deepened, running the length of her body, tautening her nerve endings. The silence surrounded them, hemming them in. She could hear the beat of her own heart, feel the movement of her blood along her veins. Moving stiffly, like an automaton, she crossed the last small space that separated them.

Below them the ground fell away into a rocky hollow, bushes and scrub clinging to its steep sides. At the base of the hollow, like a jewel in a cup, was a little ruined temple.

Few of its columns still stood intact, and the roof had gone probably centuries before. There were piles of fallen masonry all around the site of the square-raised floor, so weathered by the sun and wind that it was almost impossible to recreate it with the mind's eye and see how it might once have been. Yet, it was not forlorn. The remaining columns reared proudly toward the sky, and the bleached stones seemed to bask, smiling, in the sun.

Helen said, "It's beautiful. It's what you were telling me about in Athens—the temple to Aphrodite." Her voice was hushed and husky, her response purely emotional.

"Do you wish to go down and look more closely? There is a track of sorts, but not many people find their way here."

"That's just as well." Helen had a vision of hoards of tourists tramping down into the hollow, carving their initials on the ancient stones, sitting to eat packed lunches in the shadow of the ancient columns. Absurdly, it seemed like sacrilege. She looked at Damon. "We wouldn't cause any damage would we, if we just had a quick look?"

"I think Aphrodite will forgive us," he said and smiled at her, his eyes lingering on her upturned face, and she looked back at him, dry mouthed suddenly, her heart fluttering against her ribs like a panic-stricken bird, wondering dazedly what strange alchemy could turn the world upside down.

She thought wildly, *it's the atmosphere of this place getting to me, that's all. Nothing's changed. Nothing can change. I won't let it. We're the same people we were only a few hours ago, and I hated him then. So how can I feel that if he touched me now, I would die of the delight of it?*

Her thoughts seemed to close in on her, clamoring at the edges of her mind, bewildering her with their implications. And he was going to touch her, of course he was. His hand was reaching to take hers, to help her down toward the temple, and she stepped away from him quickly, terrified of betraying this strange, tumultuous confusion that had taken posession of her.

She tried to smile. "I can manage, thanks." Her voice was too bright, too brittle, and she saw his eyes narrow as he registered her rejection. He tossed the smoldering butt of his cheroot on the path, and ground it out under his heel. When he looked at her, the warmth in his smile, in his eyes, had gone.

"Let us go then."

The track downward could only have been used previously by goats and drunken goats at that, Helen thought breathlessly as she slithered after him in a shower of dust and loose pebbles, catching at the thick rather prickly bushes to steady herself.

The sun's warmth was trapped in the hollow, still and languid in the late afternoon. She moved slowly, feeling beads of perspiration on her forehead and mouth, but not sure whether they were caused by the heat or her heightened consciousness of the unsmiling regard of the man who sat on one of the rocks watching her as she explored the temple. There was one raised stone in the middle of the floor and she wondered if this had been the altar. It was worn and slightly hollowed out in the middle and she tried to search her scanty store of mythology to remember if the Greeks offered sacrifices to their gods and goddesses. What would be Aphrodite's price for a favor, she thought. Perhaps a pair of the birds whose cooing sounded louder than ever in this sheltered place.

She said, "Can I hear doves, or is it just imagination?"

"No, they nest near this place. You look relieved, Eleni. Were you perhaps afraid that it was the sound of Aphrodite's chariot you heard approaching? It is said it was drawn by doves."

"I didn't know that." She bit her lip. "I know so little, and yet all this is part of my heritage through my mother."

"So you admit it at last. It is, I suppose, a kind of progress. If it interests you, the statue they found stood almost where you are standing now. You can see the remains of the plinth."

"What happened to the statue?"

"It has gone to a museum, what remains of it. Why do you ask?"

She shrugged. "Just a feeling that it should be here."

"That's interesting." He lounged on his rock, and Helen found her eyes being drawn unwillingly to the strong graceful lines of his body. "The island girls would probably agree with you. For generations they came here with offerings, unbeknown to the priests, to ask Aphrodite to send them strong and loving husbands."

"How—how fascinating." There was a sudden constriction in her throat. "I—I wonder if it worked and what kind of offerings they brought?"

Damon lifted a negligent shoulder. "You would do better to ask an island girl, Eleni *mou*. But I would imagine that it was their dowries rather than any promise from the goddess that brought the young men flocking around. A girl who was not strong enough to work and bear children and whose parents had not been able to provide financially for her would find it hard to find a husband, even if she was as beautiful as Aphrodite herself. Marriage was and is a practical matter."

Helen said harshly, "Was it my mother's dowry that attracted your brother so much? I thank God that she eventually found someone who wanted her for herself alone."

He said dryly, "The match was being arranged by Michalis and my father, Eleni *mou*. I doubt whether Iorgos had any more say in the matter than your mother. But no doubt he would have wanted her. He had a way with women—too much so, or so our father thought. That is why he wished to see him safely married. And a beautiful heiress would be more likely to stop his eyes from straying after the marriage than a plain one. That is a fact of life."

"No wonder she ran away," Helen said hotly.

"Perhaps," he said. "Or perhaps she was ripe for love and Iorgos was unlucky that he did not see her before your father did. Just think, *mátya mou,* we might have been uncle and niece, you and I. Would you have liked that?"

She said stiffly, "I prefer not to have any kind of relationship with you at all."

His laugh was low and mocking. "No, Eleni? You seem very sure, and yet you are nervous of me. I know it." He came off the rock in one swift graceful movement.

Lithe as a cat—a black panther, she thought, *and as dangerous.* Her body began to tremble. She wanted to turn and run, but she wasn't sure that her legs would support her, and it was suddenly very important that he shouldn't know this. So she faced him, her chin lifted defiantly.

"Nervous of you? Why should I be?"

"Because you are also ripe for love, Eleni *mou,* and this time no other man has seen you first." His voice sank almost to a whisper as he reached her, and then it was far too late for any kind of flight because his arms were around her, drawing her against him, and his mouth was searching hers with a hunger he did not even attempt to dissemble. Her head fell back helplessly, her lips parting beneath the onslaught of his kiss. Earth and sky swung around her in a dizzying arc, and she closed her eyes involuntarily as his kiss deepened and her body melted, dissolved into pure sensation.

Her last coherent thought was that this was what she had been afraid of, what she had known she must not allow to happen at all costs, and then she was no longer thinking because instincts she had not even guessed she possessed had taken over, and her hands were sliding compulsively up to his muscular shoulders, while her mouth, mindlessly willing, responded to every intimate demand that his made of her.

His fingers found the single button on her shirt and slipped it free of its loop. The almost paralyzing grip that she had been held in slackened perceptibly, and his hand began to move on her body, his fingers circling smoothly, tantalizingly on her bare midriff, before seeking the supple indentation of her waist. His other hand moved to the nape of her neck, stroking it gently, lifting the pale strands of hair and letting them drift like silk through his fingers. Shivering with pleasure she arched her throat toward him and his mouth left hers in immediate response to explore its long curve and linger on her frantic pulse, before moving downward inexorably, inevitably to her breasts.

His hand slid down her spine, and the catch on her bikini top gave way. Helen gasped helplessly, but it was too late for protest. His lips had already brushed the narrow straps from her shoulders, and his dark head was bending to take what plunder he would.

His mouth might have been ruthless before, but it was like velvet, like silk as he kissed her breasts, his tongue tracing tiny spirals of delight on her burning skin. Her fingers twined almost convulsively in the soft thickness of his hair, and she felt an involuntary moan of pleasure rising in her throat.

The time spun endlessly, exquisitely past as Helen sank deeper and deeper into the spell of Damon's lovemaking. His hands and mouth were making havoc of all her previous imaginings of what passion could be, and she whispered his name soundlessly over and over again as her body awoke under the lingering sensuality of his exploration.

At some time—an eternity before—he had stripped off his shirt and thrown it to the ground before pulling her down beside him. She had surrendered eagerly, willingly, her hands beginning their own tentative journey of discovery.

"*Agápi mou,*" his voice was incredibly husky, his eyes dark with desire as he stared down at her. "*Se thélo polý.* I want you so much, my sunlit goddess."

Her immediate impulse was to draw him down to her, to let the wild world of the senses drown her in surrender. She knew she had never wanted anything so much in her life. She wanted Damon, wanted his arms around her, his mouth on hers as he initiated her into the ultimate ways of love. But it was as if his muttered words had broken the ring of sensual enchantment that had enclosed her, because suddenly she remembered what else he had said before he had begun to make love to her—that she was ripe for love as her mother had been before her. Would the consummation he was urging her on to be an act of love, or simply an act of possession in order to ensure that a chosen bride of the Leandros family did not escape a second time?

She said on a little gasp, "No—Damon, I—I can't. Please...." Her hands came up not to cling but to push him away as he leaned over her, a slight smile curving the harsh lines of his mouth.

He whispered, "Don't be frightened of me *mátya mou.* I'll make it beautiful for you. I'll make it beautiful for us both. You will see."

"No." There was panic in her voice. The skin of his chest and shoulders was warm silk under her fingers as she tried ineffectually to thrust him away from her, but beneath was the hardness of bone and muscle, and she was just beginning to realize how alone they were in this isolated spot, and that if Damon chose to use force there would be little she could do to resist him.

She said again, "No." And then, desperately, "There—there's someone coming. Listen."

His mouth twisted in amused skepticism as if he

recognized the age-old ploy, but he rolled away from her a little, and half sat up, listening.

They both heard it at the same moment. The tiny jangle of a bell somewhere near at hand, and seconds later, voices. Children's voices.

Damon swore furiously, then reached across Helen urgently, snatching up her shirt and bikini top and pushing them at her. Her hands were shaking so much that she could hardly cope with the fastening, but at last she was covered again, and slipping her arms into the sleeves of her shirt.

It was a strange little procession that came into view on the other side of the hollow. It was led by a nanny goat with a kid at her heels. She wore a bell around her neck and Helen found herself wondering if it was all a weird coincidence born of her own desperation, or whether she'd been aware of the sound of the bell in some recess of her mind even before it was in earshot.

Saved by the bell, she thought, and had an insane desire to go into hysterics.

The children followed. Three of them—two boys and a girl, who was wearing a dark red dress that had obviously been cut down from a garment belonging to some much older member of the family. They smiled shyly when they saw Helen and Damon, and called out a greeting in their own tongue that he returned.

Helen stole a glance at him. He had moved right away from her, and was sitting on one of the shaped stones that had once been part of a column, lighting another cheroot. He looked cool and totally in command of himself and the situation. The events of the last few minutes all seemed like some strange erotic fantasy.

Helen got to her feet. Reaction was begining to set in, and the relentless ache of frustrated desire, but even that was nothing to the sense of shame and anger that was starting to overwhelm her.

If Damon had not spoken when he did, given her time to think, she would have been his by now, totally and mindlessly. She sank her teeth into her bottom lip until she could taste blood.

So now she knew how frantically, fatally easy it was to be carried away by passion. She had not imagined she could be so easily aroused, so easily brought to the point of surrender. She had not imagined, although she had suspected, how Damon's lovemaking would overcome her inhibitions, and reduce her to eager sensuous compliance.

She thought savagely, *I don't even like him.* But the words echoed emptily in her mind, and at the back of her brain a new realization was being formed, unwanted and unwelcome but growing in strength and conviction no matter how desperately she tried to shut it out.

Suddenly she knew the truth, beyond all reason, all denial. And soundlessly she whispered to herself, *oh, God. I've fallen in love with him.*

CHAPTER SEVEN

HELEN PACED RESTLESSLY up and down her bedroom, pausing at intervals to glance at the pendant watch that she wore on a long gold chain around her neck. It would soon be time to go down to dinner, and she was frankly dreading the prospect. Because at dinnner she would have to face Damon again.

She had not spoken to him, or even looked at him after that burning moment of self-revelation in the temple. She had been too afraid that she might betray herself utterly if she did. She was too newly aware, too vulnerable to be able to mask her feelings.

So she had walked past him in silence, her eyes fixed on the uneven floor, and followed the giggling, talking children and the bleating goats up the slope and away to safety. She had been half-afraid that he might attempt to detain her, or at least to come after her, especially when the children's path diverged from her own at last, and they went off waving gaily, their white teeth flashing in cheerful grins. But the villa was in sight by then, and she was still alone, she realized with a thankful glance over her shoulder.

No one saw her as she entered the house and slipped up to her room, and she was glad of it. The last thing she wanted was for someone to notice her disheveled hair, her swollen mouth, and the dust that liberally streaked her shirt, and draw their own conclusions.

She dropped the shirt and the bikini on the bathroom floor, and stepped under the shower, gasping as the freshness of the water touched her heated body. Her skin and hair were clean and tingling when she had finished, but she had not managed to scrub Damon's touch from her body, or clear the memory of his kisses and caresses from her mind as she had hoped. As indeed she had needed to do.

It would be so easy, she thought despairingly, to simply go with the tide. To accede to whatever demands, whatever plans were being made for her without further struggle. Merely the thought of becoming Damon's wife was enough to make her body suffuse with heat, and her pulses quicken and flutter, and if all she had wanted was the gratification of her newly awakened body, then she would not have hesitated.

But that wasn't enough. It couldn't be enough, she told herself over and over again as she walked her bedroom floor. Sexual attunement was important in marriage, but it was not all-important. And what did she really know of Damon, except that he had taken command of her senses and emotions. He was just the man her grandfather wanted her to marry, because years before her mother had refused point-blank to marry his brother. This would have been a severe slight to the rich and powerful Leandros family, she could understand that. She could understand too that they would want compensation for the loss of Maria and her dowry, as well as for being made to look ridiculous, but surely the recompense could have been made in money and not in flesh and blood years later.

She had to admit that from the moment she had laid eyes on Damon Leandros, she'd had to fight her unwilling attraction to him. Had her unconscious mind been warning her even then of what her consciousness had tried to reject as ludicrous—that Damon, if he wished, could exert total and complete control over her mind, body and soul.

But she didn't want to be owned as if she was some new piece of stock to be acquired on the open market. Because that was all this marriage would mean to Damon. She had no idea of the extent of the business dealings between the two families, but she knew that her mother's intended marriage to Iorgos had been intended to consolidate this.

And now because Iorgos was dead—and not, she had every reason to believe, from a broken heart over his lost bride—Damon was prepared to take over. It was all so horribly cold-blooded—so inhuman.

She knew, of course, what the compensations would be. Damon's money to spend, travel, the kind of life other girls dreamed about. He would make love to her as and when he chose, until the novelty wore off, she thought, gnawing her lip savagely, and eventually she would bear him a child. And that, she supposed, would have to be enough. If she was honest, for many women it probably would be enough. A girl from his own country would accept the limitations of such a marriage and find her own happiness in it. But it would not be enough for her. Loving him, how could she agree to marry him, knowing the most she could hope for would be a corner of his mind, and none of his heart.

He had told her he wanted her, but he had never said he loved her. With his technique as a lover, he probably never needed to say it, she thought cynically. Craig Lassiter had said something, too, about Damon being able to have any woman he wanted, and from what Damon himself had hinted about his late brother, womanizing seemed to be a family proclivity, Helen thought unhappily.

And after the marriage, was she intended to think that all that side of his life would simply be relegated to oblivion or would Damon expect to go on playing the field in the world's capitals while she sat at home like— like faithful Penelope.

Temper rose within her, and she looked around furiously for something to smash, but she could find nothing except a bottle of her favorite scent, and she was loth to sacrifice that in the cause of bad temper. Of course, she told herself, her anger waning as the humor of the situation struck her, if she became Madame Damon Leandros, then she could have a whole row of bottles filled with the most expensive Parisian fragrances to smash whenever the fancy took her. The thought was so ludicrous that she smiled involuntarily, the smile fading as she heard a knock at the door.

She tensed, staring at the panels, as if she was trying to conjure up the face, the identitiy of the person who stood on the other side of the thick door. She walked across slowly and stood with her head slightly bent, listening for some sound. At last the knock came again.

She said in a low voice "Who—who is it?"

"It is I, *thespinís.*" The voice of her grandfather's nurse sent a shiver of relief through Helen, although this was immediately followed by a feeling of apprehension. She flung open the door.

"Is something wrong? Grandfather isn't ill, is he? He hasn't had another attack?"

"No, no, *thespinís.*" The older woman gave her a reassuring smile. "Kýrios Michalis grows stronger and more cheerful every day. I tell him that soon I shall no longer be needed here, which is a good thing for him, *ne*? I came only to tell you that he wishes to speak with you alone before you go down to dinner."

"I see." Helen said slowly. "Very well. I'll be right along."

She could have gone at once. She was dressed and ready, but she suddenly knew she had no real wish to hear what her grandfather had to say. She moved back to her dressing mirror and stared at herself, running a dissatisfied finger along the line of her cheekbone, touching the curve of her throat with scent. Finishing touches that had been added already, she scolded herself as she turned away.

Her footsteps lagged as she went along the corridor, the long skirt of her dark blue silky crepe dress whispering around her legs as she moved. The lamps had been turned on in her grandfather's room, and he was sitting in the chair by the window, staring out across the darkening sea. He turned his head and smiled at her.

"You are very beautiful tonight, *pedhí mou*."

"Only tonight?" Helen queried lightly, with a faint grimace as she bent to kiss him. "That isn't very flattering."

"It is not my flattery that you need, Eleni." There was a glint of amusement in the fierce eyes, and she felt a wave of embarrassed color rise in her face. He waved her to a footstool. "Sit down, precious child. I wish to talk to you."

Helen obeyed, sinking down rather limply on to the stool indicated, and putting up nervous fingers to fuss with an errant lock of hair. The silence stretched out, and at last she ventured to glance up at her grandfather. He had gone back to staring out at the garden, and the sea beyond, apparently wrapped in thought. It was difficult to know whether he had forgotten she was there, or was simply searching for the right words. She moved restively, and he looked down at her, his expression sad and withdrawn.

"What's the matter?" She put a hand on his arm.

"I was thinking of your mother," Michael Korialis said quietly. "You are so like her, Eleni. Will you leave me as she did?"

She stared up at him, her lips slightly parted as she

assimilated what he had said. Whatever she had been expecting, it wasn't this.

At last she said with difficulty. "Grandfather, you're not being fair. You *knew* this was only a visit. You know I have a life, obligations, at home in London."

"And what of your obligations to me? Obligations that your mother ignored when she ran away?" The old fierceness rumbled in his voice. "She was my only child. It was her duty to remain here, and face the responsibilities of her position."

"Including marriage with a man she'd never even met? Isn't that carrying duty rather too far?" Helen demanded.

"She had known since childhood what would be asked of her," he said grimly. "If I had had a son, it might have been different."

"I fail to see how."

He made a restless gesture. "A man needs an heir to carry on his business after he has gone. I built up this chain of hotels with my own hands. I wanted someone who could step into my shoes, and take the burden from me eventually. Someone tough and experienced in business. But I had no son, only a girl who spent her days dreaming her life away."

"Perhaps if she'd had some sense of purpose in her life, she would have been different. If you'd told her the running of the chain would be in her hands eventually...."

"No," he shook his head decisively. "Maria was not capable of such responsibility. Women have their own world, and it is not that of the boardroom. I needed a husband for her—a man with the right background and experience...."

"And you chose Iorgos Leandros?"

He shrugged rather defensively. "He was the elder son of my friend. There was a certain wildness, that I knew—but he was young, and his father believed that marriage would steady him."

"But it's all so one-sided. Can't you see that?" Helen appealed. "Mother must have felt like a cipher—not fit to control the business, or choose her own husband. Just expected to provide a steadying influence for a young...rake, and another heir to the dynasty in due course. No wonder she ran away. Any girl would."

"If she had not met this Englishman she would have been content enough," Michael Korialis said grimly.

"But with my father, she wasn't just content—she was supremely happy," Helen said fiercely. "And Iorgos probably wouldn't have changed at all. He might have made her thoroughly miserable."

She expected an explosion, but instead her grandfather frowned thoughtfully,

"Certainly he was a disappointment to his father," he admitted at last. "He played little part in the running of the Leandros corporation. He preferred to have a good time. But he would have been a good husband to my Maria." He banged his fist on the wooden arm of the chair. "His father and I would not have allowed it to be otherwise."

"I think perhaps they were both spared a lot of unhappiness," Helen said soberly. "Did he marry someone else in the end?"

Michael Korialis shook his head. "It was a great grief to his father," he said heavily. "But fortunately Iorgos was not his only son, as Maria was my only daughter."

Silence came down between them again, a silence pregnant with tension, then her grandfather said abruptly, "Yet I, too, am fortunate, *pedhí mou*, because I have you to bless my old age and bring me hope for the future. When I die, everything I possess— this house, the business—everything will be yours. You are my heiress, Eleni, as your mother was before you."

Helen sat at his feet as if she had been turned to stone, her eyes fixed on his face.

At last she said, "No—Grandfather, I—I don't want...."

He laid an autocratic finger across her lips. "This is how it must be, Eleni *mou*. You are my blood. There is no one else."

"There is Thia Irini," Helen protested.

"She has money of her own. Her late husband was a wealthy man. She needs nothing from me."

"And I need nothing, either." Helen felt sick. "Oh God, I wish I'd never come here. It never occurred to me...."

"Yet you knew I was a rich man," he pointed out unanswerably.

"I knew, yes, but it didn't seem to have any real connection with me. After all, we'd never met. And we're very different. We might not have liked each other. You don't have to like your relatives, after all." Helen stumbled to a halt.

There was another pause and she tried to collect her whirling thoughts.

He said softly, "How strange you are, *pedhí mou*. I thought you would be pleased. That you had realized why I sent for you."

"Then I must be incredibly naive." Helen swallowed. "This is why Madame Stavros is coming to teach me the language, and all those other things. To turn me into the Korialis girl—which is what they call me in the village already. That should have told me something. Well, go on, grandfather. Why don't you tell me the rest of the bad news?"

"Bad news?" There was a distinct air of hauteur about him. "You learn you have become an heiress, and you regard that as bad news?"

Her hands twisted together in her distress. "Not in

itself—no. But there must be strings attached. I'm just another girl as my mother was. Or has your opinion of women executives improved over the years?"

"What are you trying to say to me, Eleni?" She heard the undercurrent of anger in his voice.

"You said I was very like my mother," she said, blinking back fierce tears as she flung back her head to look him in the eye. "Well, I am, and it isn't just skin deep. I won't be used or manipulated any more than she was."

He glared at her. "You dare to speak to me in this way."

"You said my mother evaded her responsibilities. Well, I'd be evading mine if I didn't make it clear at the outset how I feel," she gave back defiantly. "I'm not a cipher, either."

The door opened and the nurse came bustling in, full of smiles, apparently oblivious to the tense atmosphere in the room.

"Dinner is ready for you, Kýrios Michalis," she exclaimed, handing him the walking stick he used to assist his progress downstairs.

Helen rose, too, glad of the interruption. The conversation between them was moving into deep waters. Sooner or later Damon's name would have been mentioned, and she could not risk that in her present vulnerable state. But at least she no longer needed to ask herself why Damon should be prepared to lend himself to this preposterous marriage scheme, she thought achingly. It was the Korialis hotel chain that he was planning to marry, and the fact that only a few hours before he had worshipped her body with his hands and mouth and called her his "sunlit goddess" meant less than nothing. If she'd been as plain as a mud wall, he would probably have behaved in exactly the same way.

Her face was brooding as she followed her grandfather into the dining room where Damon and Thia Irini were waiting. Damon held Helen's chair for her as she sat down, and she thanked him in a small polite voice, her eyes downcast, evading the searching look he gave her.

The food was delicious, but she could taste none of it, and she had no appetite anyway. Conversation was desultory at first, but what there was of it was monopolized by Thia Irini, who addressed herself exclusively to Damon with something approaching vivacity. In spite of the miserable confusion of her thoughts, Helen could almost be amused at her efforts. It was so obvious that Damon's attention was largely elsewhere, and then something she said must have struck a chord because he stiffened visibly, and she saw that he and her grandfather had exchanged a long look. But Thia Irini seemed unaware of the sudden wariness that had entered the atmosphere and continued to chat in an animated manner, her thin lips constantly smiling. But the smile faded abruptly at a barked remark from her brother, who was suddenly glowering at her, his shaggy brows drawn together.

Helen thought ruefully that those Greek lessons would have come in handy. At least she would have had some idea what was going on. As it was, no one seemed prepared to let her in on what could be the seeds of a major row, because Thia Irini was answering shrilly, her own face reddening as she spoke.

Helen glanced at her grandfather and saw that the veins were beginning to stand out on his forehead. *This is bad for him. I upset him earlier, and another argument is the last thing he needs,* she thought distressfully. To her surprise, she found she was looking across at Damon, her eyes wide with appeal, but he was already intervening, his voice low and smooth and faintly amused, defusing the situation before it got out of hand.

Her grandfather sat back in his chair, still looking displeased, but immeasurably calmer about it, and Helen smiled at him, a rather nervous placatory smile.

Thia Irini was looking mollified, as well, even a little smug. She stared hard at Helen, then said in her slow rather harsh English, "Was it good—your walk?"

Helen moistened her lips. "My walk?" she said uncertainly. Surely Thia Irini hadn't been anywhere around. If she'd followed them...Helen closed her mind to this possibility, the involuntary color rising in her face.

"To the temple." It was her grandfather. "Damon showed you the temple. Did he speak to you of the legend?"

She leaned back in her chair, her fingers restlessly playing with some fragments of bread roll left on her side plate. She said on a little gasp, "Oh, you mean the goddess Aphrodite finding husbands for the local girls. It—it sounds a marvelous idea."

And a dowry was an even better idea, she thought, as Damon himself had pointed out. A local girl would provide some land, or a house, or some stock to win the farmer or the fisherman of her choice. But the Korialis girl with her string of hotels could expect Aphrodite to drop a millionaire into her hand like a ripe plum. No limits on whatever passed for love in this part of the world for an heiress.

Thia Irini, her eyes bright with malice, said "The temple is beautiful, *ne*? You did not remain there long. I saw you go, and later I watched you return."

Using field glasses from her bedroom window no doubt, Helen thought hotly, and wondered just how often her great-aunt had spied on her. At least the temple itself would have been out of her range.

She said coolly, "I found it very impressive. It's a pity the statue of the goddess had to be removed. But I suppose it's safer in a museum. Is the temple the only ruin on the island?''

Her breasts were rising and falling too quickly within the confines of her low-cut bodice, and she forced herelf to steady her breathing, knowing that Damon was watching her, and noting her agitation.

She hoped very much that grandfather wasn't telling her they'd discovered a second Parthenon on Phoros, because she wasn't really listening to what he was saying. His voice was in the background of her mind, while all her concentration, all her being was focused on the silent figure of the man who sat opposite her, and whose hooded enigmatic gaze gave no clue to his thoughts.

The very mention of the temple was enough to fill her mind with the memory of the sun-warmed stones and the spare graceful columns against the vivid sky. Their beauty had seemed totally unreal, an encapsulated part of the pleasure Damon had forced her to experience in his arms. It was impossible for him not to remember, too—wasn't it—unless it had all just been part of a cynical charade on his part? She sent him a look under her lashes, willing him to return her glance, to let the hard lines of his mouth soften into a reminiscent curve if only for a moment.

But he was a stranger, cool and remote in his faultlessly cut evening clothes, and never the pagan who had aroused her almost to a sensuous frenzy in the burning heat of the afternoon.

And it was at that moment that he turned his head slightly and looked at her across the table. His smile was neither a sharing nor a promise. It was a cold triumphant twist of the lips, indicating that he had assessed her vulnerability and scented his ultimate victory, and Helen found herself shrinking.

The meal was at an end, and Thia Irini was rising from her chair. Helen was thankful to be able to push back her chair. The dining room wasn't small by any means, but tonight it felt positively claustrophobic.

In the *salóni*, the long windows had been opened onto the terrace, and the floor-length curtains moved in the slightest of breezes. Thia Irini was already installed on one of the low sofas pouring the dark and rather bitter coffee that Michael Korialis liked from a tall silver pot.

She held out a cup to Helen with a vinegary smile.

"Tomorrow we shall have a visitor," she said.

"Yes, I know. Madame Stavros is coming." Helen took the coffee with a word of thanks.

"No, another visitor. My—goddaughter." Thia Irini had to hunt for the English word. "Her name is Soula. She has your age."

Which must constitute the longest speech Thia Irini had made to her since her arrival, Helen thought. If it was the prospect of the unknown Soula's arrrival that had caused this thaw in the ice, then she could only wish she'd come two weeks before.

She smiled rather more warmly than she felt. "That will be lovely. I look forward to meeting her." Thia Irini accepted this with a gracious condescension of her head, and Helen seized the opportunity to escape with her coffee out onto the terrace, murmuring something about fresh air.

The night was so warm, she did not need a wrap, and the air was heavy with the scent of citrus from the nearby lemon groves. Helen put her untouched cup of coffee down on the stone balustrade. She didn't need coffee, she didn't really need air, but she did need to be on her own for a while to regain her sorely tried equilibrium.

Just for a moment back there she had let Damon see her without her defenses. She'd let her mask slip, and a far less experienced man than he was would have seen the wanting and the yearning naked in her eyes. She'd succumbed to a moment's folly, and now of course he would think he had won. That the prize was his for the taking.

She heard a footstep on the terrace behind her and tensed. She'd been a fool to think he would leave her alone for long.

She leaned on the balustrade and stared unseeingly into the darkness.

"I want to speak with you, Eleni," he said abruptly.

She swallowed. "We—we'll talk tomorrow. Grandfather will be wondering where I am. He likes me to play backgammon with him and. . . ."

"I wish to talk to you alone, now." He took her arm, detaining her as she tried to move past him toward the lighted windows of the *salóni*.

She gasped and pulled herself free. "Don't touch me."

"You sang a different song a few hours ago, Eleni *mou*. But no matter. I want to know why you left me as you did?"

She shrugged, trying to maintain at least a facade of insouciance.

"Wasn't it obvious? Your carefully planned seduction scene had failed, and I didn't want to risk a resumption once the coast was clear. You—you didn't seem prepared to take no for an answer."

"I was not," he said bleakly. "And do you honestly believe that I planned what happened between us this afternoon?"

"Didn't you?"

"If I had done," he said slowly, "there would have been no unwelcome interruptions, and that I promise you." The dark eyes were suddenly brilliant as they went over her, and Helen took a hasty step backward, her retreat impeded by the balustrade.

"Don't you dare come near me." Her voice sounded young and rather breathless and he smiled suddenly, some of the grimness going out of his face.

"And risk another interruption?" he inquired sardonically. "I think not. I ache too much already. No, I can wait, *mátya mou*. At least on my wedding night I can be sure of privacy."

His words, the tone of his voice, the way he was looking at her were all binding her in a spell that for sanity's sake she knew she had to resist.

She said, like a bright schoolgirl, "Then I hope you and your bride will be very happy. And now, if you don't mind, I really must go indoors. Grandfather will be wondering where I am and...."

His smile still lingered. "He knows exactly where you are Eleni, and he knows that I am with you."

"Another little plan?" she queried scornfully.

"If that is the way you wish to describe it."

"Well, I have other plans." She looked longingly toward the *saloni*.

"The game of backgammon? Forget it. I'm sure Michalis has. He is probably ordering champagne to be put on ice at this very moment."

She said, "Champagne. I don't understand..." her voice trailing away as she saw the amusement in his face.

"And I don't believe you. You're not a fool, my little one."

Helen stood very still. She said clearly, "Not now, perhaps. But I have been. I was a fool ever to come here—to fall for all that glib talk about family and reconciliation. Because that isn't the name of the game at all, is it?"

"Not entirely."

"That's what I thought." She smiled with her lips only. "I—I didn't know until this evening what sort of a deal you and grandfather had going, but I'd realized it must be pretty important if you were still trying to finalize it after more than twenty years. Well, I've no intention of becoming just another clause in a contract any more than my mother had. And this afternoon's demonstration hasn't affected my decision at all.''

"What is this talk of clauses and contracts?" he said slowly. "I am asking you to become my wife, Eleni."

"Oh, I'm quite aware of that," she said "And I suppose by your reckoning and grandfather's, I should be grateful even to be consulted. Of course, if you'd succeeded in seducing me this afternoon, I wouldn't even have been asked for my consent. It would have been taken for granted."

"Perhaps," he said. "But the question does not arise. You did not give. I did not take."

"Oh, please let's not talk about giving or taking," Helen said. "It's buying and selling, and we both know it. You want the Korialis hotel chain, and I happen to be part of the package. Lovely for me, of course, because you're quite a bargain yourself. Wealthy, good-looking and a marvelous lover. Quite irresistible. Only I'm not looking for bargains at the moment. Thank you for your very romantic proposal, Mr. Leandros, but no thanks. I have no plans to get married for at least the next five years. I'm having far too good a time as a single girl," she ended on a defiant note.

For a moment he stood staring at her in silence, his brows drawn together in an incredulous frown. Then he said with a quiet and deadly courtesy, "I see. May I ask if that is your final word?"

Helen swallowed. "Yes, it is. Quite final. So we don't need to pretend anymore—either of us. You—you don't have to play the great lover where I'm concerned any more." She was being deliberately wounding, hurting herself equally by the insolent words. "I'm sure you have far more rewarding ways of spending your time, and people you'd rather spend it with. That dark-haired beauty who was in your car that day in Athens, for instance. She would probably be more than glad of some attention. You've been neglecting her lately.'' She stopped, hearing the authentic ring of the jealous woman in her voice, and terrified that he would recognize it, too. But he was too angry.

"Thank you for your gracious permission," he bit back at her. "I won't hesitate to avail myself of it. What a pity you didn't accept my proposal, Eleni *mou*. What an understanding wife you would have made."

"Men like you don't take a great deal of understanding," she said with cold bitterness, and held herself rigidly waiting for some kind of storm to break. But after a moment he turned away, and she closed her eyes in sheer relief, sagging back against the balustrade.

She had sent him away, which was what she had known she must do, so why did it hurt so much? But she knew the answer to that almost before the question had formed in her tired brain. It hurt because he hadn't even bothered to deny what she had said. All the time she had been speaking, accusing him, her mind had been screaming silently, "Tell me it's not true. Tell me that you'd want me if we were strangers who'd only just met, and I wasn't the 'Korialis girl.' Tell me the past never existed, and that you love me, and I'll believe it because more than anything in my life, I want to believe it."

But he'd said nothing, and his silence confirmed everything she had suspected and feared, everything that rumor had suggested.

But the knowledge that she was right gave her no satisfaction, only a pain as deep and abiding as the dark and whispering sea itself.

CHAPTER EIGHT

HELEN WAS WAN and weary-eyed when she awoke the next morning. And Josephina, after a swift tactful look at her pale cheeks and shadowed eyes, rustled off to bring back her breakfast, with the insistence that she should remain in bed to eat it.

Helen was only too glad to accede to the suggestion. She even managed a smile for Josephina as the tray with its complement of coffeepot, fresh orange juice, and oven-warm bread with red-currant preserve was laid across her knees. She wanted none of it, but she had to make a pretense of eating as Josephina bustled around the room, clicking her tongue in slight reproof as she bent to pick up the discarded crepe dress from the floor. Helen felt guilty as she watched. She wasn't usually so untidy, but last night she had been totally uncaring as she had pulled off her clothes and tumbled into bed. She hadn't even bothered to clean her makeup off properly.

I'm a mess, she thought candidly as she sipped the refreshing tartness of the orange juice, *both physically and emotionally.*

It had taken all the courage she possessed to walk back into the *salóni* the previous evening, but to her relief the room's only occupant was Thia Irini, hunched over her everlasting tapestry work. She'd sent Helen a sly darting look as she entered, but had said nothing. Helen didn't need to inquire where her grandfather had gone. He and Damon had obviously withdrawn to somewhere more private to discuss this new obstacle to their plans, and she had no wish to wait around and hear what conclusion they had come to. Not that she had any illusion that it would concern her. She had made herself more than clear on that point.

She stifled a groan as she remembered just how clear she had been. Damon's face, his eyes had frozen as he looked at her. He was an arrogant man, used to succeed. Her rejection of him would be a blow to his pride that he would never forget or forgive.

She crumbled a piece of bread roll in her fingers. But it had been that or the total surrender of her own pride. And Damon would soon find consolation, she told herself desolately.

Josephina was chatting cheerfully and inconsequentially as she tidied the room, and Helen forced herself to listen to what she was saying and respond suitably. The servants at the villa must have a shrewd idea of what was in the wind. Servants always did have, she suspected, and she didn't want the chatter to say that she was quiet and lovelorn.

Last night as she tossed and turned trying to sleep, she had decided the best thing she could do was ask for a seat to be booked for her on the next London plane out of Athens. But now in the clear light of day she was not so sure of this. On purely practical grounds, this was the height of the holiday season and she might well have difficulty in obtaining a ticket anyway. There would be no private jet for the homeward journey, she thought with a wry smile, remembering the way she had come to Phoros from London, and wondering how she could have been so blind. Even then she'd been fighting her attraction for him, she thought, only she hadn't fully realized how vital it was for her to win that particular battle. And in the end she had lost all the way around.

It would have been so easy last night to tell herself that the desire she saw in his eyes was love. But how long could that sort of deception last within the ultimate reality of marriage? Until he became bored, she supposed, recalling the cynical regret he had expressed the previous evening about losing such a potentially understanding wife. *That's what he thinks,* she told herself, her hands instinctively balling into fists. *I would not be understanding at all. Why, if he so much as looked at another woman, I'd—* she stopped abruptly, forced herself to relax and take a sip of her rapidly cooling coffee. That particular train of thought was singularly unproductive. If she was going to be able to get through the remainder of her stay at the villa without betraying herself, then she would have to keep away from the thorny areas of what might have been.

She became aware that Josephina was watching her, an expression of concern on her wrinkled face, and she forced herself to smile.

"How—how is Kýrios Michalis this morning, Josephina? Have you heard?" She wasn't too worried. If the previous evening's events had caused any kind of relapse, she was sure she would have heard already.

As it was, Josephina's smile positively beamed. "He is well, *pedhí mou,* how should he not be? Your being here has made him so happy. Everyone speaks of it."

"I'm glad of that. I—I shall miss him when I have to go home."

"Go home?" Josephina sounded aghast. "What talk is this? Kýrios Michalis does not expect that you will go home."

"I think I know what Kýrios Michalis expects," Helen said in a low voice. "Nevertheless I shall be returning to England at the end of the month."

"But—child of my heart—what of Kýrios Leandros?"

"What of him?" Helen retorted more calmly than she actually felt. "He is no concern of mine, Josephina."

"No concern," Josephina almost wailed. "But *pedhí mou....*"

"Could we change the subject?" Helen appealed hastily. She glanced around her. "Why are you doing my room, Josephina? Isn't that Yannina's job?"

"*Ne, thespinís,* but with a guest arriving today, she has another room to prepare, so her duties are mine." Josephina's tone was suddenly more formal, but her dark eyes, as melancholy as a monkey's, could not conceal her bewilderment as she looked at Helen.

She thinks I'm mad, Helen thought moodily, thrusting the almost untouched tray of food away from her. *Probably I am. I've just been offered half a loaf and I prefer to join the ranks of the starving.*

Presently Josephina took the tray, and still rather formal in manner, excused herself. Left to herself Helen found the prospect of a shower a positive enticement. She felt sticky and aching after her restless night. She made to push away the concealing sheet, and paused as a knock came on the bedroom door. She smiled wryly. Josephina was really holding aloof. Normally she knocked and entered in one movement, chatting volubly as she did so.

Helen called, "Come in," and rolled across the bed to the side table, reaching for her wristwatch.

The door opened, and Damon came in.

For a moment she was too stunned to move, then she snatched frantically at the slipping sheet, cursing herself silently because she'd fallen into bed the previous night without bothering with a nightdress. And the fact that he himself was immaculately dressed in a lightweight cream suit with a dark brown silk shirt and tie only served to make the whole situation that much worse.

"What do you want?" she gasped.

"There is no need for such panic," he said coolly. "I have not come here to force myself on your unwilling body. Not even my overwhelming greed for your grand-father's possessions would prompt me to rape. I am going to Kyritha to meet the ferry, and I wondered if you wished to accompany me."

"Can you think of a single reason why I should?" Helen tried to slide unobtrusively down the bed, but the sheet was becoming wound too tightly and revealingly around her body to permit much movement.

"Oh, yes. Your companion and tutor Madame Stavros is arriving, and I thought you might wish to be the first to greet her."

"Oh," she said rather weakly, unwilling to confess that the events of the past twenty-four hours had dismissed Madame Stavros's imminent appearance on the scene from her mind. "Of course, that's who Yannina was preparing the room for. I—I didn't realize."

"Madame Stavros's room has been ready for some time. The activity this morning is to prepare accommodation for Kýria Irini's goddaughter who is also due today."

"Yes, she mentioned it yesterday. I didn't know she was expected quite so soon."

"Neither did anyone else, including your grand-father. She broke the news to him at dinner last night," he said rather dryly.

"Oh, is that what it was." Helen recalled the slight fracas. "He wasn't at all pleased, was he. Doesn't he like her?"

Damon lifted one shoulder in a shrug. "I don't think he cares much for her. Last night the prospect of having her here as a guest did not appeal to him at all. This morning, he is a little more reconciled. Well, do you wish to come with me to Kyritha or not?"

She flushed slightly "I...don't think so. I have a slight headache, and being cooped up in a stuffy car won't really improve it."

"What has happened to last night's honesty, Eleni? It is myself that you do not wish to be 'cooped up with,' is it not so? No doubt you wish that I would remove myself from your vicinity altogether, but I regret to say you will be disappointed. I am having alterations done at my own villa, and it is not convenient for me to leave your grandfather's house. We are both his guests here, and we can at least be civil to each other."

"Well, I still don't wish to come to the village with you," she said between gritted teeth. "I've no burning urge to meet Madame Stavros anyway. Her coming here is a complete waste of time."

"Under the circumstances, perhaps," he agreed levelly. "Nevertheless I hope you will extend the civility I spoke of to her. She is an old friend of both our families."

"Butter," she said equally levelly, "will not melt in my mouth. Does that satisfy you?"

"I think we will not discuss any of the ways in which you might satisfy me." His voice was silky. "I doubt whether you would wish me to enumerate them."

Helen's face flamed. She said shakily "Just—get—out." But she was talking to the door gently closing behind him. She turned convulsively onto her stomach, and buried her face in the pillow.

THE MORNING was dragging endlessly, Helen thought as she threw another pebble restlessly into the sea. The villa seemed to be in uproar over the expected guests, with Thia Irini everywhere hectoring the impassive servants into cleaning again already immaculate rooms. Helen had wondered rather wryly whether the same fuss had been made prior to her own arrival. Not that she grudged the unknown Soula any of it. She knew that in Greece the relationship between godparent and godchild was a particularly close and important one, and if having Soula as a guest at the villa pleased Thia Irini, and did anything to improve her temper, then Helen was all for it.

She had paid her usual morning visit to her grandfather in some trepidation, but his reception of her had been calm and affectionate. Damon's proposal and her rejection of it was not even mentioned, and that was odd, she thought, bending to select another pebble. Perhaps her grandfather decided that it would cause less embarrassment all around if everyone pretended the whole thing had never happened. She swallowed painfully, thinking, *some hope of that.*

It was all very well for Damon to talk of being civil, because the next week or two was going to be the most difficult of her life, and civility didn't even enter into it. She was heartsick, and at all costs she had to conceal the fact. She tried to encourage herself with the reminder that with other guests staying at the villa, close encounters of any kind with Damon would be easier to avoid. A little bitter smile twisted her lips. Who was she trying to fool? If the villa was bursting at the seams with happy holidaymakers, she would still be conscious of him and only him with every fiber of her being.

Moodily she swung back her arm, and threw the pebble as far as it would go. It was then she saw the boat nosing its way around the headland. It was a caïque, and Helen assumed it was one of the local fishermen. She'd seen plenty of them sail across the small bay during her long leisurely hours on the beach. But this boat was not sailing across the bay, it was turning toward the shore and, as Helen watched, its sole occupant waved to her. Puzzled, she shaded her eyes, staring at it. The villagers knew this beach was private. Surely they wouldn't land here unless they were in trouble, and the soft put-put of the boat's engine sounded healthy enough. The fisherman waved again, and shouted something that sounded amazingly like, "Helen." As the boat came nearer she realized that he had fair hair, and that it was Craig Lassiter.

Hastily she slipped off the cheesecloth tunic she was wearing over her bikini, and kicked off her sandals. Then she ran into the coolness of the water and struck out for the boat.

It was farther out than she thought and she was breathless by the time Craig was bending to help her out of the water and over the side.

He said smiling, "Welcome aboard, fair Helen. The other nine hundred and ninety-nine ships are following. I could only manage to launch this on my own."

She laughed and accepted the towel he handed her, wringing the excess water out of her hair.

"What brings you here?"

"The most beautiful beachcomber in the Aegean." His eyes were frankly admiring as they studied her and she flushed a little, draping the towel over her shoulders. "I met you, and I wanted to see you again. Don't tell me it's an uncommon reaction."

"I don't think I need tell you anything," she said dryly. She looked around. "Is this your caïque?"

"No, it belongs to a friend, but I have the use of it when I want."

"You obviously have very obliging friends."

"I'm good to them. They're good to me," he said airily. "And how is life in the Korialis household?"

Had his gaze become slightly more searching, Helen wondered. "Much as ever," she said.

"But I thought your future husband had come down from Mount Olympus or wherever such godlike beings reside, and was staying at the villa."

Helen bit her lip. "If you mean Damon Leandros— yes, he is there. But he is not, and never will be my future husband."

"You make that sound almost official."

"It is," she said shortly. "Be the first to know."

Craig stared at her for a moment, then gave an appreciative whistle.

"You mean you've actually turned the great man down. Oh, but that's wonderful. That's made my day."

"I can't see why it should have done." Helen found his exuberant reaction perplexing. "Do you actually know Da—Mr. Leandros?"

"He doesn't exactly put me at the top of his guest list," he said sarcastically. "But I know him, naturally. He's my landlord."

"Your landlord? Then you don't own your *taverna*?"

"Hell, no. Very few of these waterfront places actually belong to the people who run them. They're rented, usually from rich Athenian businessmen. You're pretty safe normally, unless your particular waterfront gets caught up in the tourist boom, and the landlord decides your *taverna* would make more money for him as a gift shop or a boutique or a smart restaurant. It happened to a friend of mine on another island. Next thing he knew, his rent had gone sky-high and he had to get out."

"But that's dreadful."

"It's business," Craig returned dryly. "But fortunately the tourists haven't discovered Phoros to any great extent yet. Not that that's stopped Leandros trying to get rid of me in the past on a number of occasions."

"Why should he wish to do that?"

Craig shrugged. His face was sullen suddenly. "Pressure from an old friend, perhaps. I did say that your grandfather hadn't been very well disposed toward the English up to now. Having me living in Kyritha must have been like a red rag to a bull."

"Well, the whole thing makes me feel very ashamed," she said hotly.

"No need." He sent her a lazy smile. "I can cope, I

promise you. In my own way, I can be just as stubborn as any of these Greeks.''

Helen returned his smile, but she felt uneasy for no apparent reason, and a slight chill went through her that wasn't prompted by damp skin and hair.

Craig noticed. "You're cold. Here, I've got a sweater in this bag.''

She said, pulling it on, "It's always colder out on the water. I'd forgotten that.''

It was far too big for her, of course, the wide cowled collar standing away from her slender throat, the sleeves hanging below her fingertips. Helen pushed them up her arms, aware suddenly that in contrast to the thick texture of the wool, her long honey-tanned legs looked exotically smooth and bare. She felt more exposed than when she had climbed into the boat wearing nothing but a wet bikini, and that was ridiculous. She gave her hair a brisk rub with the towel, asking questions about the caïque. Did Craig use it often? Could he sail it, or did he always use the engine? She was aware of the nervousness behind her chatter, although she could not altogether understand it. Craig was pleasant. She'd enjoyed his company in the village, and it was flattering that he had deliberately sought her out so soon, but that was all there was to it.

And she was grateful to him for his company. She hadn't enjoyed being alone with her thoughts on the beach.

She was grateful, too, when he produced a packet of food—rolls filled with cold roast lamb, slices of smooth creamy cheese, and a bag of fresh peaches. The air had given her an appetite.

"That was wonderful,'' she said licking peach juice from her fingers. "Can you always produce instant picnics for hungry beachcombers?''

"It could be arranged. Do you come to the beach every day?''

She hesitated. Her remark had been intended to be a lighthearted one. Not an invitation or a hint that this morning's meeting should become part of a pattern. She looked at him and saw him smiling ruefully.

"You think I'm being pushy?"

"No, of course not," she denied rather too hastily. "But I'm not too sure of my plans at the moment. I could be returning to England almost at once."

"I see." He looked downcast at the prospect. "Well, I suppose it's inevitable. It isn't likely that a mere *taverna* keeper would stand a great deal of chance with the Korialis heiress."

She felt a surge of irritation. "Helen Brandon's the girl you need to bother about, and I don't go in for outdated snobbery. If I stay around Phoros, then I hope we can become friends. I—I might need a friend."

"My pleasure." He smiled at her. "Now how do you fancy a few hours sailing—a conducted tour of Phoros from the sea?"

"It sounds very appealing. But I think I really ought to be getting back to the villa, we're having guests and I. . . . Oh, hell—" she broke off. She'd turned to look at the beach, and had seen the dark figure standing at the water's edge, holding her discarded tunic.

Craig followed her gaze. "The rejected suitor?" There was a note of malice in his voice.

"That same." She stood up biting her lip. "I expect grandfather is asking for me. I really will have to go. Thanks for the lunch and the loan of the sweater."

She stripped it off and handed it back.

"You should keep it," he said. "It does more for you than it ever did for me."

She laughed. "I don't think whoever went to all the trouble of knitting it would be very pleased. Well, I'll be seeing you."

His hand was on her bare shoulder, and he was stand-

ing very close to her suddenly. "I hope so," he said softly, his breath warm on her ear. "I really hope so,
Helen."

And what that would have looked like from the
shore, she couldn't imagine, she thought miserably as her body cut through the water. Behind her
she could hear the caïque's motor splutter into
life. Craig had presumably decided that discretion
was the better part of valor. She stood up in the
shallows, and began to wade forward with care because
the seabed was covered in stones, and walking over
them was difficult and could be painful. She could
only manage one swift glance at the man who was
waiting for her, but that was all that was necessary. He
looked bleak with rage, his lips drawn into a thin line.
When she reached him, he threw the tunic to her word-
lessly.

"Thank you," she said coolly, her heart hammering
and her pulses jumping uncontrollably. "Have—have
you been waiting long?"

"Long enough," he said on a snarl. "What were you
doing with Lassiter?"

"Talking. Sharing his lunch. Wearing his sweater."
She sounded flip, but inside she was fainting. "If you
hadn't turned up, we'd have gone for a sail around the
island."

His hand closed around her arm, his fingers biting
into her flesh so deeply that she had to stifle a cry.

"You will go nowhere with that man. Do you understand Eleni? Nowhere."

"No!" She tore herself free, and stood glaring at
him, tension spiraling up inside her at his touch, even in
anger. "You don't own me. I'll go where I wish. See
anyone I want. Do *you* understand?"

"And you want Lassiter?" His mouth curled in deri-
sion.

No, she thought in pain. *I want you, and I love you. How can you put your hand on me and not know it?*

"I might," she lifted her chin, sensing that her best defense lay in defiance.

He uttered an expletive under his breath and turned away. She found her discarded sandals and followed him. He did not look around at her or speak all the way back to the villa, and she trailed miserably in his wake through the garden. There were voices ahead of them, and she hesitated. Her tunic was clinging damply to her body, and her hair was sticky with salt and hanging in rattails. She didn't really want to be presented to visitors in this state, Helen thought, wondering whether she could slip into the house unnoticed.

But the decision was apparently not hers to make. Even as she paused, Damon turned, and before she could protest, he had taken her arm and was urging her inexorably forward toward the steps that led up to the terrace from the garden.

They were all there. Her grandfather, Thia Irini, a small rather plump woman, very fashionably dressed, who could only be Madame Stavros, and a girl.

She was slim, and very dark, her glowing rather insolent beauty offset by the dress she was wearing—a couture creation in orchid pink silk. She looked the epitome of confident chic, and Helen by contrast felt more appallingly scruffy than ever as she reluctantly mounted the steps beside Damon

Madame Stavros was rising with an encouraging smile, her hand held out, but while Damon was performing the introduction, Helen was aware that the girl was watching her. She glanced toward her, catching the newcomer off guard and saw an unmistakable flicker of resentment in the dark eyes, before the long mascaraed lashes descended to hide it.

Helen thought, *she doesn't like me. But that's ridiculous. We've never even met. Or have we?*

She had the oddest feeling that she had seen her before somewhere. A memory was teasing her, that she couldn't clarify.

"And this is Soula, Soula Markos," Damon said, and the girl turned her head slightly and smiled up at him, her glance flicking disdainfully past Helen.

And then Helen remembered where she had seen Soula before. It was the lift of the head, the smiling profile that jogged her errant memory.

Athens, she thought. *She's the girl who was with him in Athens.* She saw the manicured hand slide confidingly over Damon's arm, saw the slight provocative sway of Soula's body toward his—and saw Damon look down smilingly into her eyes, the bleakness wiped from his face. Pain tore at her. She said huskily, "I—I think I'll go and change if no one minds."

No one did, it seemed, but then they were all far too busy watching Soula and Damon. Approving smiles all around, even from grandfather, Helen thought as she went into the house.

I'm not going to be able to bear this, she told herself despairingly. *But I must. I can't complain about anything he does. I told him I didn't want him. I told him to find consolation. But it never occurred to me I'd have to watch while he did.*

She was shaking like a leaf when she reached her bedroom. She closed the door behind her, and stood for a moment, trying to steady her breathing, trying to hang on to her self-control.

Aloud she whispered, "I had to do it. I couldn't have married him, knowing it was only part of a business deal, and that he didn't love me."

But she knew she was wrong. She knew now, too late, that she would rather have married Damon, even knowing he was indifferent to her, than know this agony of seeing him with another woman.

She said, "Too late." And then her face crumpled like a child's and she began to cry.

CHAPTER NINE

HELEN CLOSED the textbook she had been studying and pushed it away with a yawn. So far in the ten days since Madame Stavros had joined them at the villa, she had managed to master the Greek alphabet, and had learned a number of useful conversational phrases, but she doubted whether she would ever acquire the ability to chatter away in the language.

Yet she was enjoying her lessons and Madame Stavros's company more than she had ever dreamed possible. At least she had something to occupy her mind and keep her from brooding, and someone who could distract her attention from the fact that Damon and Soula were spending every waking minute together.

They might be sharing other moments, as well, Helen sometimes thought when she saw them together. Soula was usually demure when Thia Irini was present, but Helen had seen the way she looked at Damon sometimes, and doubted cynically whether the lovely Greek girl was half as innocent as she liked to give the impression of being.

But whatever the truth of the relationship, Thia Irini obviously thought it was going to end in marriage, and the prospect was making her purr like a contented cat. She lavished attention on Soula, and Helen began to understand why the older woman had been so hostile to her when she arrived. Thia Irini had always intended that her goddaughter should be Damon's bride. Helen's appearance on the scene had provided a hiccup in her plans.

Helen wondered sometimes whether Madame Stavros had guessed her unhappy secret. She was not only charming and cultivated, she also seemed very warm-hearted and Helen was often tempted to confide in her. But so far she had managed to restrain the impulse, reminding herself that Madame Stavros was an old friend of the Leandros family, as well as of Michael Korialis, and might feel obliged to pass on the news that her charge was eating her heart out for the man she had refused to marry. Certainly being with Madame Stavros made it much easier to avoid Damon and his new companion than it would have been if she'd been hanging around the villa on her own. Madame Stavros enjoyed swimming so the daily visits to the beach had continued. One afternoon they had driven into the hills for a picnic, and they had twice been into Kyritha to do some shopping. On one of these occasions they had passed Craig's *taverna,* but he had been nowhere in sight. There had just been a rather tired-looking girl doing some sweeping. Perhaps he was out in the caïque looking for more beachcombers, Helen had decided with a faint smile. In a way she was relieved that he wasn't around because she was sure that Madame Stavros would have had her instructions.

Soula, fortunately, disliked the beach so Helen was spared the sight of Damon dancing attention on her there. The Greek girl was finicky in the extreme about her personal appearance, and spent hours each day changing her clothes, which Helen had to admit were exquisite. If she had brought any beachwear with her to Phoros, then she kept it a closely guarded secret, and Helen couldn't imagine her in anything as informal as a swimsuit or bikini, with her immaculate hair damp and tousled. In fact Soula very rarely ventured out of doors at all, preferring the shade of the pergola when she did so. One hothouse flower, that lady, Helen thought rather caustically.

But as a millionaire's wife she was probably tailor-made for the job. She looked the part already, and Helen could only pray that the actual engagement would be delayed until she was safely back in England.

She would have to return soon. The last letter from Hugo had contained a slightly plaintive note. He was missing her, she knew, and back on her own ground, in her own familiar circumstances, she might find Damon a little easier to forget, or so she hoped. It was, after all, almost all she could hope for.

She got up restlessly from her seat in the pergola, and began to wander along the terrace. She could hear the murmur of voices from the *salóni*. Her grandfather was there, she knew, playing chess with Damon. Soula wouldn't be far away, either, her head bent over that everlasting embroidery she had brought with her. Helen paused at the French windows and looked in at them. The family party, she thought with a little stifled sigh. And I'm the outsider.

Michael Korialis glanced up and saw her. "Come in, *pedhí mou*. Ariadne was looking for you just a moment ago. She intends to drive into Kyritha. Do you wish to go with her?"

"Yes, I think I will." Helen advanced into the *salóni*, conscious that Soula had glanced up and awarded her white sleeveless blouse and dark green cotton wrap-around skirt, with its enormous bow just over her left hip, zero out of ten for chic and allure. Soula herself was wearing crepe de chine in pastel colors, with delicate spike-heeled sandals. For someone who was actually quite robustly built, she managed to exude an air of helpless fragility, Helen thought and gave herself a mental kick for being spiteful.

She forced herself to smile at the other girl. "Would you like to come with us, Soula? You've hardly seen the village."

"What is to see?" Soula lifted a shoulder in a graceful shrug. "It is a small village. There is nothing there of interest."

"Perhaps you and Eleni are interested in different things," Damon said. He had not looked at Helen since she entered the room, and he did not look at her now. All his attention seemed concentrated on the chessboard and his next move.

He means Craig Lassiter, Helen thought, feeling an angry flush steal into her cheeks. She said with a deliberate drawl. "Actually I find Kyritha has a fascination all its own. But I couldn't expect you to understand that."

At that he did look up. "On the contrary, I understand very well," he said, and the contempt in his eyes made her flinch. Muttering something about finding Ariadne Stavros, Helen made her escape.

It appeared that the afternoon's jaunt was in search of some tapestry wool. Greek women seemed to have a passion for fancy work of all kinds, and Kyritha boasted a shop selling canvas, wools, embroidery silks, transfers, cushions and tablecloths. Helen couldn't figure out where all the customers came from, but it seemed to do a roaring trade. Every house on the island must be dripping with hand-embroidered table runners and wall hangings.

Madame Stavros's speciality was tapestry cushions, and she made her own designs and patterns, using beads and glitter threads to add extra life and color. She'd offered to teach Helen, but she'd declined albeit reluctantly. She'd had this ridiculous vision of herself and Soula spending the long summer evenings stabbing needles through their respective patterns, and wishing they were stabbing each other.

Kyritha was crowded, and Kostas had to park the car some distance from the shops. The embroidery shop was packed when they reached it and Madame Stavros made a little face.

"I shall have a long wait, it seems. Perhaps I should leave it for another day. You will be bored, my dear child."

"I can always go for a stroll," Helen said. "We can meet later at the *kafenion*."

She saw the palpable hesitation, the indecision in Madame Stavros's face, and sighed. "I haven't any assignations planned."

"I am sure you have not," *madame* assured her. "You are a good child. But not everyone is as good." She gave a brisk shrug. "Go along then," she said. "We will meet in twenty minutes."

Helen wandered along the waterfront, dodging between the laughing chattering groups of holidaymakers, and avoiding the solemn row of small boys edging the harbor wall with their fishing rods. She could see *Phaedra* riding at her moorings, and the sight of her made Helen's heart turn over. She had thought there could be nothing worse than the humiliation she had suffered at Damon's hands on board *Phaedra*. Well, she knew differently now.

She was deliberately walking away from Craig's *taverna*, so it was sheer bad luck that she should almost bump into him. She smothered a groan. Madame Stavros would still be lining up for her tapestry wool, but Kostas would be around somewhere, and no one would believe she hadn't planned this meeting.

He said, "Surprise, surprise. I thought you were back in England."

"Don't tell me the local grapevine has broken down," Helen said sarcastically.

"Oh, it's still operating, but now it has the all-conquering Mr. Leandros paired off with another lady. He's a fast worker, I'll give him credit for that.'' Suddenly he was brimming with resentment, and she looked at him in surprise. "Not two days after he saw us together, I got a letter from his lawyers in Athens pushing the rent for the *taverna* through the bloody roof. There's no way I can pay it, and he knows it. Business has never been that wonderful. The Greeks can be very clannish, especially on Phoros.''

Helen said hotly, "But that's dreadful. It's your living. What are you going to do?''

He shrugged. "Get out and make a new start somewhere else, where his shadow doesn't fall.''

She said, her voice shaking, "I'm sorry, Craig. I'm really sorry.''

He nodded. "It'll teach me to be careful about the caliber of my future enemies. Perhaps I'll see you again before I leave.''

"Are you leaving soon?''

"Within the next day or two.'' He grimaced slightly. "I suppose I should be flattered that he thought me a risk. But he was way off target, wasn't he, Helen? I fancied you, but you didn't fancy me.''

She flushed. "This is hardly the time or place. . .'' she began, and he nodded again, patting her arm.

"Be seeing you,'' he said and went on his way. She watched him go, and while she couldn't summon up a great deal of regret, she felt burdened by guilt. She'd deliberately implied to Damon that Craig might be important to her, when she knew perfectly well there was not a grain of truth in it. If she'd never spoken to Craig, never shared his lunch on board the caïque, he might still have his *taverna*, she thought remorsefully.

She was shocked to her heart's core at the pettiness of Damon's revenge. It was unforgivable—like taking a sledgehammer to kill a fly. It would soon be time to meet Madame Stavros at the *kafenion*, and she hadn't the slightest desire for a cup of coffee. She wanted to return to the villa and confront him with what he had done.

It was torture to have to sit under the awning of the *kafenion* and admire the tapestry wool, and marvel at the exactness of the match, and some of her answers boarded on the distrait, causing Madame Stavros to glance at her sharply.

She was so quiet on the homeward journey that Madame Stavros eventually asked her if she was ill.

"A slight headache, that's all."

Madame Stavros tutted, laying a cool and scented hand on Helen's forehead. "When we reach the villa, you shall lie down and Josephina will bring you some herb tea."

Helen said with false brightness, "That sounds wonderful."

She didn't want herb tea, although some Dutch courage might not have come amiss. Either that or a copious drink from Lethe—the waters of forgetfulness.

She wanted to be able to pull down a blind in her brain, wipe out the last few weeks as if they had never been. She felt scarred emotionally, but the scars would fade in time. Christopher might help—if he was still waiting around, which she doubted. After all, she'd barely given him a thought since she left London. But if not him, there would be someone else.

She went straight to her room on reaching the villa. The downstairs rooms were deserted. Everyone had gone up to change for dinner. Josephina appeared at once, and insisted on helping her take off her blouse and skirt. Helen submitted to her ministrations, and put on her white broderie-anglaise housecoat, promising to wait quietly on her bed until the herb tea was produced.

As soon as the coast was clear, she slipped out of her

room and ran on bare and silent feet to the corridor, where her grandfather's room was situated. Damon slept in a room in this corridor, too, at least officially, Helen thought bitterly as she knocked quietly on his door.

He called, *"Peráste."* He must have thought it was one of the servants.

Helen opened the door and went in. For a moment she thought her ears must have deceived her because the room was empty, and then he came out of the bathroom. He'd clearly just had a shower. His hair was wet, and his sole garment seemed to be a toweling bathrobe loosely belted around the middle.

He stopped dead when he saw Helen and his dark brows drew together in a frown.

"An unexpected pleasure, Eleni," he said in a voice that conveyed not the slightest hint of pleasure.

She swallowed. "I have to talk to you," she said rapidly. "I heard today that you'd done a rotten thing, and I have to tell you that you're wrong. I let you think I was interested in Craig. . .to—to annoy you because I knew you didn't like him very much. But he means nothing to me."

"I am relieved to hear it." He shrugged, his tone bored.

"Is that all you've got to say?"

"What more do you expect?"

"But doesn't it make any difference to you—to your attitude to Craig?"

"None at all." He was silent for a moment, then he said quite gently, "You flatter yourself, Eleni, if you can imagine my actions over Lassiter were prompted by jealousy. I was concerned that you might become involved with him, I admit, but my decision that he must leave Phoros was taken long ago."

Helen said, "I don't understand."

"No, that is true. You have never understood. You let yourself believe that both Michalis and myself were blinded by prejudice over Lassiter." His voice was even, but it stung. "And, of course, he was your countryman. It was perhaps natural that you should wish to think well of him, and badly of those villainous Greeks who see human life as an entry on a balance sheet—or a clause in a contract."

"I didn't know him well enough to think well or badly of him," she said frankly. "He was pleasant to talk to, that was all. There was nothing else to it. You have to believe that."

"I believe you. And I am glad of it. You have been saved a great deal of misery. Christina, of course, was not so fortunate."

"Who is Christina?"

"His wife."

"What?" It came out as a yelp. "He's—married?"

Damon nodded. "To a girl from Kyritha. How else do you suppose he acquired the *taverna*? He did not know, of course, that Christina's family only rented it. He supposed it belonged to them. He saw it as a meal ticket for life. Her father was dead, and her mother warned her about Lassiter, but she would not listen— for good reason. She was pregnant."

"He has a child, as well," Helen said slowly.

"No. The child died shortly after it was born."

"How awful."

"For Christina, yes. Lassiter knew little about it. He was off on a drinking and fishing trip with one of his friends. The funeral was over when he returned."

Helen said, "There was a girl at the *taverna* one day, sweeping the floor."

"That is Christina. She was very pretty once. Now she works every hour of the day so that he can spend the profits on drink and chasing other women." He paused, then said dryly. "It is as well he is leaving Phoros, for his own sake. He has come very close to being lynched by angry fathers in the past. The island can do without a man like that, so I gave my lawyers certain instructions. They took longer to act on them than I had expected, and unfortunately you met him. Kostas was very upset. Lassiter had tried to seduce his sister, so his family had sent her to stay with an aunt on Hydra."

"You mean Kostas thought that Craig would try to seduce me?" She was going to say, "Oh, but that's ridiculous," and then she remembered how she had felt on the caïque.

"He has no love for either your grandfather or myself," he said. "He would probably have found it very amusing to seduce you."

"That's revolting," she said shakily.

"You would possibly have found it so," he agreed. He picked up his watch from the bed, and fastened the gold bracelet around his wrist. "Now if you will excuse me, I would like to dress."

"Yes, of course." She moistened her lips with the tip of her tongue. "I—I'm sorry I said what I did just now."

His lips twisted sardonically. "You have said so many things, Eleni. One more makes little difference, believe me."

She did believe him. His eyes, his tone of voice, everything about him proclaimed his supreme indifference, and she wanted to fling herself at his feet and weep.

But instead she smiled and nodded brightly and said, "Well, I'll be going. I won't be down for dinner. I have a headache."

"I have some aspirin, if you wish them."

"No, no," she said, still with that insane brightness. "Josephina's going to dose me with some herbal tea. I shall be fine. All I need is a good night's sleep." She smiled, and got herself out of the room somehow.

Josephina was waiting with a glass in a silver holder when Helen got back, and she began to scold, but after a swift look at Helen's white face and quivering lips, she set down the glass and took the trembling girl in her arms. She asked no questions, and suggested no answers, and presently, when the first storm of weeping was past, she put Helen to bed as if she was a child, and fussed over her gently until she drank the tea down to the last drop.

Whatever was in it, it worked. Helen was asleep almost before she knew it.

And then she was awake and the room was full of moonlight, flooding in through the window, swamping the bed. The moonlight was drawing her to the window, to the balcony outside and she went willingly, lifting her face to the great silver orb that hung in the sky over the sea. It made a shimmering avenue across the water, and she was leaning forward, trembling a little, waiting for what might be.

The whisper of the sea was getting louder, its note changing so that it sounded like the murmuring of a thousand doves. And then the doves were there, a great flock of them, wheeling and circling in a white and fluttering cloud, and in the middle of the cloud a chariot shaped like a silver shell, carrying a girl with hair like spun foam, and eyes as dark blue as the Aegean itself.

Helen thought incredulously, *Aphrodite, the foam-born one. But it can't be. It's not possible. No.* She cried the last word aloud, and woke to find herself sitting bolt upright in bed in a room filled with moonlight.

She said shakily, "My God, Josephina. That herbal tea packs quite a punch." She threw the sheet back and got out of bed because the moon was making the room as bright as day, and further sleep was impossible unless she closed the shutters and drew the curtains.

She was awake this time, and she knew it, and she'd seen the effect of moonlight across water before, but she lingered for a moment just the same admiring the effect and recalling the vividness of her dream. It had been so real. Real enough to make her wonder even now whether, if she went to the ruined temple, the empty plinth where the goddess had once stood would now be occupied.

She shook her head in self-mockery at her own fancifulness and went back to bed. But this time sleep eluded her. It was too warm with the shutters closed, and she tossed and turned restlessly, seeking a cool place on the pillow.

At last she sat up and said aloud, "This is ridiculous." And it was. She wanted to rest, she needed to sleep, because then she didn't have to think, and there was a lot she would have liked to forget. If she could close her eyes she might dream again—not of pagan goddesses rising out of the sea—but of a man who looked at her not with bleak indifference, but with love, and whose mouth curved sensuously as he whispered her name and buried his face in her hair.

She muttered, "Oh, Damon," on a little groan, and lay alone in her wide bed and ached for him, and for all the dreams that would remain unfulfilled in the years ahead.

She thought, *I should have married him when I had the chance. I should have taken him on his own terms. He wanted me, and perhaps in time I could have made him love me. If I'd had his child, he might have loved me then. Greeks adore children.*

And she saw him with Soula in image after agonizing image, until her nerves were screaming, and her body felt like fire, and there were tears pricking and smarting behind her eyelids. She couldn't breathe, the room seemed to be closing in on her, and beyond the shutters the moonlight beckoned.

She kicked the sheet away and slid to the floor. In the clothes cupboard, she found a pair of jeans and a sweat shirt, and pulled them on. There would be no one around to see or disparage her unfeminine attire at this time of night. She carried her sandals in her hand, moving silent and barefoot through the sleeping house. Downstairs the main door wasn't even bolted, and it yielded noiselessly as she tried the handle.

The gardens were strange in the moonlight, stripped of their vibrancy and color. She moved through a silver landscape down to the silver sea.

Helen stood at the water's edge, letting the small waves ripple and cream around her feet. The night was warm around her, but a slight breeze blowing off the sea was fresh on her face, and she inhaled thankfully.

She thought, *tomorrow I'll go to grandfather and tell him he must let me go home—go back to England. At least there I won't have the torment of seeing Damon, of watching him with Soula. And I'll tell grandfather I don't want his money. I've learned to love him, and I'll come back and see him if he wants me to, but I don't want to be an heiress. It's spoiled everything.*

Dropping her sandals on the beach, she bent and dipped her hands in the water, pressing the cool drops against her flushed cheeks. Then, acting on an impulse she barely understood, she dragged her shirt over her head, and unzipped her jeans, letting them drop to the ground. She waded into the sea up to her waist, then lowered herself fully into the water and began to swim with long steady strokes. She did not venture too far out. After all she was alone, and the water was cooler at night, and she did not want to risk an attack of cramp.

The moonlight surrounded her and lifted her up. She

turned onto her back and floated, moving her hands lazily, the radiance of the night bringing her a kind of peace. She thought that on a night like this she could believe in anything, abandon all touch with reality. She could even believe that a girl whose name still symbolized all the beauty and the passion of a pagan world could rise up out of the sea in a silver shell. She could understand the faith of the island girls who came stealthily by night to her ruined shrine to ask for a chance of happiness that, after all, was the least anyone could ask for.

And she knew what she had to do. She swam unhurriedly back to the shore along the path of moonlight to where her clothes were waiting. They felt clammy and uncomfortable being pulled over her damp skin, and she was probably asking for an unpleasant chill if not pneumonia, but it no longer seemed to matter. She thrust her feet into her sandals, and ran up the beach and through the rustling olive grove. She slowed a little when she found the track to the temple. The last thing she wanted was to sprain her ankle on one of the loose stones.

She had nothing to offer, of course. She was wearing no rings, no chains or pendants. Even her watch was back at the villa. She hoped Aphrodite was in a generous mood and would take the will for the deed.

She was breathless as she reached the top of the slope and looked down into the hollow, and it wasn't just because she'd been hurrying. Just for a moment she'd wondered whether she would look down into the temple and find she was not alone. She was being a fool, of course, and she knew it, but twentieth-century rationalism skated lightly across the surfaces of places like this, and race memories and superstitions ran deep, and she was doing a very superstitious thing. Hugo who had vaguely humanistic leanings would never believe this, but she thought her mother might have understood, and smiled a little. . . .

She slid the last few yards in a flurry of gravel and dust, then walked across the floor of the hollow and climbed up on the first of the great stone slabs that formed the base of the sanctuary. She took a deep breath and moved forward a few paces, then halted, holding out her palms upward in the age-old gesture of the suppliant.

She whispered, "I love him. Please let him love me. Please send him to me."

Then she waited while the silence enfolded her.

But only for a moment. Even as she released her pent up breath in a little sigh at her own foolishness, she heard it. The rattle and scrape of a pebble falling down the slope, dislodged by a careless foot. Her whole body stiffened with tension, and her hands flew up to cover her trembling mouth as she tried to bite back a scream.

Damon's voice said from the shadows at the edge of the sanctuary, "I frightened you. I'm sorry."

Helen's eyes widened incredulously, and she took an instinctive step backward as he stepped out into the moonlight.

She said stupidly, "But—what are you doing here?"

"I followed you. I could not sleep, and I saw you leave the villa, so I came after you."

"And—watched me?" Her face warmed as she remembered how she had walked naked out of the sea.

He bent his head silently in affirmation.

"You're despicable."

"I am human," he retorted. "When I got to the beach, I thought you had vanished, and then I saw you swimming. I stayed in case you got into difficulties. If you expect me to apologize for looking at you, then you will be disappointed."

"Oh, I expect nothing," she said bitterly. "But your

future wife might not be to happy about the situation. Not that she'll ever learn about it from me. I'm going back to London as soon as I can persuade grandfather to make the arrangements.''

"And if he cannot be persuaded to let you go soon?''

"Then I'll get to Athens somehow and ask the consul for help," she flashed. "My father will send me the fare home when he knows I'm stranded.''

"You are really so desperate to get away?''

"What do you think?''

"Where you are concerned, I no longer know what to think," he said savagely.

Helen bit her lip, "Then it's just as well I'm leaving," she said quietly, and a little shiver ran through her. Part of it was caused because she was still damp from her swim, but some of it—most of it—was because she felt desperately forlorn.

Her prayer, if that's what it had been, had been answered. Damon was here, but nothing had changed. They still faced each other as antagonists, and she could really have expected little else.

"I—I'd like to go back to the villa. I'm cold," she said, and at once he unslung the jacket he was wearing over his shoulders and took a step toward her. His intention was obvious, he was going to put it around her. His hand would touch her, brush her skin, and she knew she couldn't take that. She might burst into flame, break down, weep, beg for his love. She said quickly, "I'm all right," at the same time stepping backward and putting out a hand to ward him off.

He stopped in his tracks, his face grim, his dark eyes accusing.

He said, "You won't even accept this much from me. Yet that day on the caïque you were wearing Lassiter's sweater. I saw you return it to him. Is this perhaps why

you are leaving in such a hurry? So that you can leave
with him?''

''No.'' The very thought appalled her. She had
forgotten about Craig lending her the sweater, but
she remembered it now, how it had been hand-knitted
with evident care, and how little he had seemed to
value it. She supposed Christina, his wife, had made
it for him. It had been a complicated pattern with a lot
of work in it, and a lot of pride, and probably a lot of
love, and in retrospect it all seemed unbearably poi-
gnant.

''Yet you're crying for him,'' he said bleakly.

''Like hell I am. I was thinking about his wife, if you
must know. What will happen to her?''

''She has relatives here, she will be looked after,'' he
said, and Helen believed him. He didn't have to enlarge
on the subject. Christina had made a mistake, and if her
own relatives still blamed her for this, he would provide
any necessary protection.

''I'm glad,'' she said. ''She's better off without
him.'' She saw his mouth twist cynically, and hurried
on. ''I really mean it. I told you Craig meant nothing to
me. He—he was a stranger.''

''A stranger? Yet you drank with him in public, spent
time alone with him on a caïque in the bay, actually
came to me to plead his cause.''

''He told me that you and grandfather were preju-
diced against him because he was English, among other
things. He was very convincing.'' She looked at him
steadily. ''But I'm not going away with him. You have
to believe that.''

Their eyes met, and held, but after a moment he
shrugged. She knew what the shrug implied. It meant he
believed her for what it was worth, but it was no longer
important. She was no longer the girl he intended to
marry, so she could behave as indiscreetly as she chose.

Soula, on the other hand, would probably never give him cause for concern.

He said abruptly, "Why did you come here tonight?"

"I was cold after my swim. I needed exercise," she said feebly after a moment. "And I wanted to say good-bye to the temple."

"Wouldn't daytime have been a more appropriate time for a visit?"

"I'd already seen it in daylight," she said and pressed her hands to her flaming cheeks as she remembered the exact circumstances of that afternoon. "Now please may we go back to the villa?" She needed to change the subject. Damon had been following her, he must have watched her from the top of the slope as she stood here making her futile, pathetic appeal to the nonexistent. It would be humiliating beyond all bearing if he guessed what she had been up to.

"As you wish." He fell into step beside her. "Michalis will be grieved that you wish to go so soon."

"It isn't really that soon," she protested. "I was only ever coming for a month. And I'll be back to see him again."

"When?"

She thought, *when you're away and gone, and I can be sure I won't have to meet you and your wife.*

She shrugged, "Sometime. I—I'll write to him, of course."

There was silence. They'd reached the edge of the sanctuary, not moving fast when Damon said, "Would it make any difference to your decision to leave if I told you his lawyers were coming to Phoros next week?"

"No, it wouldn't." The exclamation was almost a cry of pain. "I don't want to know about that. I'm content with what I have, to be what I am. I don't need a chain of hotels, or to be an heiress. I don't want it. It's spoiled everything."

She had stopped, and he turned her to face him, his hands gripping her arms. He said, "Michalis only wants you to be happy. That is all he ever wanted. He thought that I could make you so. He still thinks it. That is why he has agreed to sell the Korialis chain to the Leandros corporation. If the deal goes through—if it is truly what you want—then you will no longer be an heiress, Eleni *mou*. I thought then that I would ask you again to marry me."

Helen swallowed. She was still asleep. She was dreaming. She must be.

He said huskily, "Look at me Eleni, *mátya mou*, my eyes, my precious one. Speak to me. Don't torture me like this."

She said on the merest breath of a whisper, "But the hotels—the money...."

"I don't need them, *agápi mou*. I need you as I need breath in my body." He pulled her forward into his arms, and his mouth found hers for an endless reeling moment.

At last he lifted his head and looked down at her. He said, "From the first moment I saw you in your father's gallery, that's how it has been with me. How could you not know?"

She shook her head, hardly daring to believe what she was hearing, to let the delirious joy welling up inside her to overwhelm her.

"But it was all arranged. Grandfather wanted us to marry because—"

"Because of your mother and Iorgos? No, my heart. I swear he never thought of it until I asked him for you. The negotiations over the hotel chain had been going on for months before. They were held up because of his illness. Then when he knew I wanted you for my wife he decided to make the hotels and everything else that he had your dowry." His smile was rueful. "He thought it would please you. That it would suit your English independence to know that you would not be coming to me empty-handed.''

"You never told me you loved me," she said slowly.

"Not in words, perhaps, but then I had only just begun my wooing, and you were so determined not to let me near you—except that afternoon when I brought you here.'' He gave an unsteady laugh. "I knew then that I could not trust myself to be alone with you, and that we must be married as soon as possible. What I did not know was that Michalis intended to tell you that he was making you his heiress, so that any proposal from me would have sounded completely mercenary and calculated. Your grandfather and I came nearer to a quarrel over that than at any time in our lives. He is of a different generation, *agápi mou*. To him a woman is property like a house or a piece of land. He thinks we are both mad. And of course, there was the other alternative.''

"What alternative?'' She slid her arms around his neck, smiling into his eyes, deliberately provocative, loving the way his arms tightened in response, the pressure of his hard body against hers.

He smiled. "That you didn't want me, in spite of everything your body was telling me, and that you were using your accusations simply to get rid of me. Or even that you wanted the money more. There was always that possibility, too. After all, you still have not told me you love me. *M'agapás?*''

She said shakily, "I can't say it in Greek, Damon, my lessons haven't got quite that far. But I love you with all my heart.''

He said softly, "We won't embarrass Madame Stavros by asking her to teach you love words. I prefer to tutor you myself.'' He lifted a strand of her hair and brushed it across his lips. "*Se thélo polý,* Eleni *mou.* I want you very much.''

"And I want you," she whispered, lifting her mouth to his, her body melting against his.

When she could think again, she said, "Were you jealous of Craig?"

"I am jealous of everyone you speak to and smile at," he said. "Kostas was anxious. He said you talked much together, and that you smiled a great deal."

"I noticed him disapproving," she said wryly. "But Craig never stood a chance, even if he was the island Romeo. I think I must have been in love with you then, although I didn't realize it. But I'd told myself so often that I hated you because of the way you'd treated me, and made a fool of me, that I had to believe it." She paused. "And then, of course, there was Soula. You were with her that day in Athens."

"I have been with her on many days in Athens, usually bearing messages from Kyria Irini. Your great-aunt was endlessly inventive in devising little errands that would bring us together. Inviting the girl here was an act of desperation, I think. She knew how angry your grandfather would be." He smiled reminiscently. "I was intended to see how altogether more suitable Soula would be as a bride."

"Is that really all there was in it? There was nothing more between you than that?"

"Nothing, *agápi mou*. I was content to flirt with her, if by doing so I could obtain some reaction from you." His eyes glinted wickedly down at her as she made a muffled sound of protest. "But Soula's heart is still untouched, although her vanity may be a little dented when we announce our betrothal. She will make a suitable marriage. You need not worry about her."

"Is she an heiress?"

"Yes. Almost as rich an heiress as you, my precious one. And she would not relinquish one drachma of it for any man walking the earth."

"Money is such a responsibility," Helen said. "And don't laugh at me, Damon, you're used to it. It's all very well for you. Will grandfather be very hurt, do you suppose, because I don't want this inheritance?"

"I think he will recover," he said sardonically. "He intends to discuss with his lawyers the possibility of setting up a trust fund of some kind for our children. He is as stubborn as you are, *agápi mou*." He took off his coat and wrapped it around her. "Now we will go back to the villa, Eleni, and in the morning we will tell him that we are going to be married, but not, I think, about tonight's escapade. It would only worry him."

"It would convince him we were mad." She smiled. "Perhaps I was a little crazy. I didn't come here to say goodbye. I came to ask Aphrodite for you, even though I didn't have anything to leave as an offering."

"No offering was needed," he said gently. "I was yours already. Since time began, and until it ends." It was like a marriage vow.

She said, "Since time began, and until it ends, Damon *mou*." And lifted her mouth for his kiss.

An exciting new series
of early favorites from

Harlequin Presents

This is a golden opportunity
to discover these best-selling beautiful
love stories — available once again
for your reading enjoyment...

because Harlequin understands
how you feel about love.

Available wherever Harlequin books are sold.

Make 1981 your best year yet!

——— with ———

Harlequin Romance Horoscope 1981

★

How to find your most compatible mate!

★

When to plan that romantic rendezvous!

★

How to attract the man you want!
And much, much more!

Choose your own special guide—
the book for your zodiac sign.
Find the way to love and happiness
in the coming year!

PLUS Romance
Calendar 1981
A special guide for those in love!

Harlequin Romance Horoscope

Available now at your favorite store!

FREE!
Romance Treasury

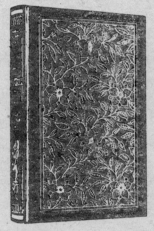

**A beautifully bound,
value-packed,
three-in-one
volume of romance!**

FREE!

A hardcover Romance Treasury volume
containing 3 treasured works of romance
by 3 outstanding Harlequin authors...

...as your introduction to Harlequin's
Romance Treasury subscription plan!

Romance Treasury

...almost 600 pages of exciting romance reading
every month at the low cost of $5.97 a volume!

A wonderful way to collect many of Harlequin's most beautiful love
stories, all originally published in the late '60s and early '70s.
Each value-packed volume, bound in a distinctive gold-embossed
leatherette case and wrapped in a colorfully illustrated dust jacket,
contains...
- 3 full-length novels by 3 world-famous authors of romance fiction
- a unique illustration for every novel
- the elegant touch of a delicate bound-in ribbon bookmark...
  and much, much more!

Romance Treasury

...for a library of romance you'll treasure forever!

Complete and mail today the FREE gift certificate and subscription
reservation on the following page.

Romance Treasury

An exciting opportunity to collect treasured works of romance! Almost 600 pages of exciting romance reading in each beautifully bound hardcover volume!

You may cancel your subscription whenever you wish! You don't have to buy any minimum number of volumes. Whenever you decide to stop your subscription just drop us a line and we'll cancel all further shipments.